D0399005

The Hedgehog of Oz

Also by Cory Leonardo

The Simple Art of Flying

The Hedgehog of Oz

CORY LEONARDO

Aladdin
New York London
Toronto Sydney New Delhi

This book is a work of fiction. Any references to historical events, real people, or real places are used fictitiously. Other names, characters, places, and events are products of the author's imagination, and any resemblance to actual events or places or persons, living or dead, is entirely coincidental.

ALADDIN
An imprint of Simon & Schuster Children's Publishing Division
1230 Avenue of the Americas, New York, New York 10020
First Aladdin hardcover edition February 2021

Book designed by Tiara Iandiorio
The text of this book was set in ITC Stone Serif Std.
Manufactured in the United States of America 0121 FFG
2 4 6 8 10 9 7 5 3 1
This book has been cataloged with the Library of Congress.
ISBN 978-1-5344-6759-0 (hc)
ISBN 978-1-5344-6761-3 (eBook)

For Caleb, Sam, and Amelia

May you always find your way back . . .
Back to the road that leads you home.

Overture

TUCKED BETWEEN A BRICK APARTMENT BUILDING and a busy corner deli, on a storybook tree-lined street, sits a theater. A run-down but beautiful theater.

At precisely six o'clock every morning, a long ladder pushes through the shiny front entrance, and with a wrench and a terrible screech, the ladder unfolds. Under the cheerful glow of the marquee, an elderly man ascends.

One by one letters are plucked from beneath the NOW SHOWING sign and scooted around. *Attack of the Atomic Alien-Cats* becomes *Night of a Thousand Kisses* in the bat of an eyelash. Though the marquee might read *Marigold Takes Manhattan!* at 6 a.m., by

6:05, *Bleak Battle III* will blaze in its stead, lit up by the hundred globe lights that hug the edge of the great sign and wink on the cracked tiles below.

A ticket booth, all glass and gold trim, stands waiting between two sets of doors, ready to collect dollar bills, coins, traces of pocket lint.

And every evening, tickets in hand, the moviegoers file in with anticipation. Past the doors. Into the lobby. Through the warm, inviting balm of buttery popcorn air.

A line forms at the snack counter. Orange Fizzy Pop and Crystal Cola sloshes into tall cups of ice. Popcorn pops in an old-fashioned popcorn cart and spills into greasy buckets; stray kernels crunch into the carpet below.

The cash register chimes as a woman in blue orders Chocolate Buttons and gummy Fruit Gems, while a gaggle of small boys presses noses and sticky fingers to the smudged glass. They ogle long ropes of licorice and lollipops the size of their heads. A pair of elderly gentlemen order the same confection selections—Coco-nutties, Toffee Beans, and Cinnamon Snaps—three boxes each. Gumdrops, peppermints, caramels so sticky they can't be carved from your teeth for a week—the register sings and sings and sings.

Past the concession stand, deep inside and so high it seems pinned to the clouds painted on the peeling ceiling, a heavy curtain cascades to the stage and pools in great crimson tufts. (It harbors more than a few moth-eaten holes.) And though it's a bit worn now in places, the theater's proud gold paint brightens the baseboards, the balcony, the flying monkeys spiraling up pillars to the opera seats, a cornice of poppies crowning the stage. Emerald City murals, chipped and faded over the years, glow from the wings, while the theater's threadbare velvet seats warm under the sparkle of diamond chandeliers.

All is hushed. Everything waits . . .

CRASH-CLONK. The lobby doors open.

People stroll down the aisles and plunk themselves into seats—two here, three over there.

Chandeliers dim as tiny glass bulbs bordering

the aisles flicker to life, lighting the way for more napkins, a splash of soda, a second bag of licorice.

The music strikes its first chord. Voices hush.

The curtain rises.

And the show goes on.

The theater's heart beats differently every night. The screen might conjure a laugh, a gasp, even an infrequent snore. A sob might bubble up and float into the rafters.

Squeals of fright. Peals of delight. It's just like this that the months and years of the Emerald City Theater have marched on. And from gleam and sheen to wear and tear, the decades slowly drifted by.

There is one thing, however, that has always remained the same.

Every Saturday at noon sharp there plays one matinee show.

The film hasn't changed. The same movie reel clicks away every Saturday and has for as long as anyone can remember the doors being open.

And lately, something else, too.

A small pair of eyes has been glued to the noon matinee each week. A pair of eyes, behind a pair of much-too-large eyeglasses.

Kansas. Flying houses. A group of travelers on the yellow brick road. Every Saturday, high in the theater's sagging balcony, now closed off and cobwebbed with time and disuse, a bespectacled Marcel perches on the back of a dusty theater chair, taking it all in. The Wicked Witch cackling and the film reel crackling. Those ruby slippers and "no place like home."

Marcel knows every word of "Over the Rainbow." He's sung it probably a thousand times.

Well, *before*. Before he came to the theater, that is. Once upon a time.

He hasn't sung a note of it since.

For a while, as the first violin notes quivered to life and his beloved moving picture lit up the screen, he could still imagine it, though. A reunion. One fit for the movies.

A happily ever after.

Maybe she'd seen the marquee. Maybe with a

hitch in her heart and Marcel on her mind, she'd decide to take in the show—their show—one more time.

And for a while, he'd watch. *Not* the matinee. But for that glimpse of braids, the flash of braces, a sticker-covered skateboard. For a long time, months even, a glimmer of hope remained.

But she never came.

And now?

Well, Auntie Hen might perch beside him. And when she's not pecking at a popcorn kernel or the sticky remains of a lemon drop, Uncle Henrietta will sit for a few. Two fat hens, roosting in the balcony above a dark theater, watching *The Wizard of Oz*.

And Marcel, that Oz-loving hedgehog?

Yes. He watches too.

CHAPTER 1

The Limes

MARCEL LISTENED AS GOMER DUPREE wrapped up the day's battle against the old janitor's sworn enemy: bubble gum. Blobs on the metal trash baskets, wads under seats, globs stuck like growths to the flying monkeys carved into the pillars.

When the last wad was vanquished, Gomer (getting on in years and stooped with arthritis) valiantly vacuumed candy and popcorn kernels from the seat cracks and scrubbed what soda pop glue he could from the floor. He missed some things.

When Gomer came back in after changing the marquee, Marcel perked up his ears.

The old man grabbed his empty thermos and keys, stepped outside into the dark cloak of early morning, and locked the glass doors. There'd be quite a few hours before he'd return for tonight's showing of *Dragons of the Deep: A Love Story*.

When at last the theater was quiet and Gomer Dupree was safely away, Marcel scrambled up the broken railing of the balcony and popped his nose over the edge. He gave the air a good sniff.

Ah. Breakfast.

"Two Licorice *Twithsts* under seat 26D, a small bag of popcorn behind the trash bin—nearly full—and one lime Fruit Gem stuck to the exit sign in the north wing. I think there might be a yogurt raisin near the restrooms too," Marcel said proudly. (He might depend on a strong pair of glasses—hedgehogs have terrible eyesight, particularly with the chandeliers dim, as they were now—but boy could he sniff out a yogurt-covered raisin when he needed to.)

But where *were* his glasses?

Marcel looked away from the fuzzy sea of seats below and back into the balcony. He didn't like creeping up on the sisters when they were still sleeping, so he cleared his throat and tried again.

"We could probably do without the Fruit Gem, huh?" he asked, squinting at the green mountain of lime gummy candies piled in a corner.

He was met with silence.

His *glasses*. He needed them in order to get started, and . . .

He'd just remembered where he'd seen them last.

Marcel coughed into his fist and raised his voice a hair. "Auntie Hen? Uncle Henrietta?"

Auntie Hen, who'd been snoozing in the seat next to Marcel's overturned popcorn tub of a house, in a nest made from a blue cashmere cardigan she'd plucked out of the lost-and-found box behind the concession stand, stirred, flapped her wings, and stretched. "Lime," she clucked. "They always leave the lime ones! No one ever leaves a strawberry."

"That's true," said Marcel as he scrambled to the row in front of Auntie and poked his nose between two seats to squint at her. He could count on his paws the number of times they'd come across a coveted strawberry Fruit Gem.

"Now, why do you think that is, dearie?"

Two seats over, Uncle Henrietta opened one eye. "Because the lime ones taste like grass, that's why."

"They do taste a bit leafy," said Auntie Hen, eyeing the mountain of lime candies in the corner and shaking her head.

"Like grass!" replied her sister.

"Don't forget about the yogurt raisin and Licorice Twithstssss," said Marcel.

"The what?" said Auntie.

"The Licorice Twithstssss," said Marcel. Auntie Hen frowned.

Marcel had a voice the hen sisters said reminded them of the slush machine in the lobby—sloshing, a bit wet. S's always seemed to get caught in the back of his mouth and shimmy before they squirted out.

He said it slower this time. "Lic-or-ice *Twithstsssssssss.*"

"*Licorice Twists!* He said *Licorice Twists*!" shouted Uncle Henrietta. She took one look at Marcel. "And where are your glasses?" she barked, before turning her head and plunging it into the coppery feathers of her back.

Auntie blinked. "*Oh!* Marcel! What's happened to your glasses?"

Marcel pointed behind her and blushed.

"Well, how did they get there?" said Auntie, turning to find his spectacles wedged beneath her feathery behind.

How indeed. But eyeglasses of all sorts had a way of turning up in many a seat. Marcel had often thought that his, found stuck between seats 93 and 94A after a Saturday matinee, were like a gift from the Good Witch Glinda herself. From the moment he'd put them on, everything was crisper, brighter, *Technicolor*. The world looked like a bit of Munchkinland magic with the right pair of glasses.

It took a good amount of tugging and clucking, but Marcel's spectacles were soon retrieved. He adjusted them on his furry nose.

Auntie Hen beamed at him. "Don't you look dashing."

"He looks like a horsefly," came Uncle Henrietta's muffled grumble.

Marcel smiled at his friends. "Good morning, Auntie. And good morning, Uncle Henrietta. How was your sleep?"

"Terrible," said Uncle.

"I've had better," Auntie mused. "I think a chunk of plaster got me right in the head last night. Barely slept a wink!"

On trying mornings such as these, Marcel usually volunteered to scrounge up breakfast alone. Even when fully rested, the hens were slow. They might get distracted by a petrified gummy worm and peck at it for hours. They'd stop to catch their breath and fall asleep in one of the seats and Marcel would have to start a one-hedgehog search party. And then there was that time Auntie Hen caught a claw in the carpet, lost her footing, and rolled down the entire length of the grand staircase, end over feathered end, landing in a heap at the bottom, a gumdrop wedged in one eye.

It wasn't a pretty sight.

"You can rest if you're not feeling up to it today," he said.

"Up to it?" Uncle Henrietta repeated. "You try balancing on a couple of straws for legs and then ask me if I want to climb stairs."

"I can get your breakfast. I don't mind," Marcel assured her. And he didn't mind. It kept him busy, kept his mind off, well, *things*.

Okay, it kept his mind off *her*.

Dorothy. *His* Dorothy.

Auntie Hen waved a wing in his direction. "No, no, Marcel. You can use the assistance. And *we* could use the exercise. We'll help!" She leaned close and winked. "If my dear sister didn't insist on stuffing herself with so many Toffee Beans, her legs wouldn't be such a trial.

"Can't blame her, I guess," she went on. "I've

acquired quite a taste for Cinnamon Snaps myself. I can't tell you what a relief it is not to be eating chicken feed for every meal."

It wasn't a year ago that the hens had arrived. And on a howling storm of a night.

The French film *Bonjour, Mes Amis* had played that evening (*Hello, My Friends*, the subtitles read); Marcel always thought it a serendipitous wink of fate. The hens were the *only* visitors who'd laid foot or claw in the balcony since Marcel arrived. Even Gomer Dupree gave the abandoned, not-quite-safe and never-needed-anyway balcony a blind eye.

The hens had escaped from a poultry truck crammed with cages, awhirl with flying chicken feathers, and bound for a warehouse. What a warehouse *was*, they couldn't be certain, but Uncle Henrietta always had a good gut instinct about things and felt they didn't want to find out.

Into the broken air vent in the alley, they went. Through a maze of metal tubing—left and right and up, up, up. Landing finally in the balcony by way of a missing heating grate, the same twisty path Marcel had taken . . . Was it more than six months ago now?

Had it really been more than six months since then? Since . . .

Marcel shook his head to chase the thought away.

The sisters had tumbled into the balcony with a wet crash and a flop, rolled down an aisle, and come to a stop at the balcony's edge, thunder heralding their arrival.

And Marcel had barely been able to contain himself. He'd held out a paw, just like he'd seen people greet each other in movies. (His was a tad shaky with excitement.) Spouting a hundred hellos, he'd asked for their names.

The first chicken blinked at him. "Sister," she'd said.

"Sister," Marcel repeated. "And your name?" he asked the second.

"Sister," said the other. "She calls me Sister."

Marcel had frowned. "You're *both* Sister? Don't you have names?"

"Since when does a hen need a name?" the second chicken had asked. "Don't see why it matters."

But to Marcel, it did. "I might like to tell you apart better," he answered her. "Do you think I could give you names?"

"Of course you can!" said the first chicken.

"Don't see why it matters," repeated the second.

But two names popped into his head then. From his favorite movie, *The Wizard of Oz*.

Auntie Em. Uncle Henry.

Those were names he could work with.

He'd looked to the first chicken. "Can I call you Auntie *Hen*?"

"It's perfect!" she'd said.

He looked to the second. "And, you, maybe Uncle Hennn . . . rietta?"

"Fine," she'd answered.

And fine it fairly was and had been ever since. For two old hens who'd never seen anything more than the inside of a cage their whole lives, the Emerald City Theater was a pretty good gig: room to stretch, plenty of snacks, and the movies weren't bad either.

But to Marcel, their arrival meant he was no longer alone.

He'd always be a bit lost, mind you, but at least now he wasn't *alone*.

Marcel, listening to Auntie peck at her sister to get moving and Uncle squawking her displeasure in reply, wandered back to the balcony's ledge. He climbed up, rested his chin on the mahogany, and peered into the empty seats below.

Alone.

It was surprising that for all its beauty, for the cheery show tunes and happy endings, for the many smiling faces it welcomed and friendly whispers soft as a kiss, a place like the Emerald City Theater could still feel very lonely. He'd seen it in the face of an old woman sitting in an empty row, dabbing her eyes during *Summer's Loss*. She'd left before the movie ended.

He'd seen it in a boy with his mother on

opening day of *Sea-Space 9: Intergalactic Octopus Invasion*, stealing glances at a group of kids his age. When the group spotted him, they'd pointed fingers, whispered, snickered. The boy had slouched deep in his seat, trying to disappear.

Marcel knew lonely feelings well.

Sure, there were things he supposed he liked about living in the theater: The smell of popcorn, heavy in the air and clinging to the patchy carpets. A caramel when he could find one. He found himself getting swept up in every romantic movie and trying to imagine what it felt like to have an arm around your shoulder or someone holding your hand. He loved when children came for the cartoons; the sound of their excited babble was as soothing as a scratch behind the ears. Marcel liked it when they laughed at the funny parts. He laughed at those parts too.

And then there was *The Wizard of Oz* every Saturday.

It had been their movie—his and Dorothy's.

His Dorothy's.

He remembered the first time he'd stepped into the theater, and there it was playing! Hope had swelled in his heart like a hot air balloon.

It was a sign! It was something. If his Dorothy fell from the sky anywhere, surely, *surely*, she would fall right here. And then maybe everything could go back to what it was. *Maybe?*

He thought he'd found her again so many times.

The flash of red high-tops might do it. A glimpse of auburn braids. If a girl with freckles on her cheeks and braces on her teeth walked down an aisle, lowered a seat, and settled in with a tub of popcorn with extra butter, he only saw her.

His long-lost Dorothy.

But visions like that tended to melt as quickly as slush from the slush machine, and hope gets tossed away as sourly as folks tossed out their Fruit Gems.

It was always, always the limes.

CHAPTER 2

A Peppermint Predicament

THE DIFFICULT THING ABOUT SATURDAYS WAS timing.

After he locked the glass doors of the freshly groomed theater on the heels of a Friday-night show, Gomer Dupree would walk home to get a few hours' sleep before returning to open for the Saturday matinee. For the three stowaways, this meant little time to glean the treats that were kicked under the soda fountain or stuck between seats. Overlooked popcorn kernels could be found every which way, but it took hours to gather them, and drinking from the soda machine was a lot harder than it looked. They had to take turns pressing the buttons. And though hopping down the sweeping staircase wasn't too taxing on the hens, when they *did* join Marcel, climbing the steps back to the balcony was no easy task. There were more than a few times they'd made it back to row HH just as the janitor's key turned in the lock.

This particular Saturday was turning out to be just such a day.

"Hurry up, Hen," grumped Uncle Henrietta. "Your legs are as long as mine and I'm twice as wide. There's no excuse for the snail's pace."

An out-of-breath Auntie lagged behind, trying to balance the rare find of a half-full box of Fruit Gems on her wide back. "Sister," she wheezed. "You forget I'm older than you. There's less life in my bones."

Uncle Henrietta snorted. "Twelve hours isn't older, you old biddy. Get a move on."

Marcel pulled the box from Auntie Hen's back. "Need some help?" he asked. "You could spear a few on my spines. They're sure to stick."

Auntie Hen smiled. "Well, now, there's a plan," she said, and together they skewered eight limes, a lemon, and two particularly precious strawberry-flavored Gems, to his left shoulder, right flank, and the top of his head.

"You look like a Christmas tree!" Auntie said when she was done. (Auntie had a fondness for any film with a Christmas tree in it, as they looked "good enough to eat.")

"Hrmph," grumped Uncle Henrietta from the doors to the lobby. "You're going to look like a *deserted* Christmas tree if you don't hurry it up!"

Marcel rushed up the theater aisle and out into the lobby toward the steps to the second floor. Auntie huffed and puffed behind him.

Day had dawned while they'd been getting breakfast, and outside the theater's glass doors, the sky had the gray tinge of cold weather to come. Marcel wondered if he shouldn't summon the small, retired freight elevator; he regularly encouraged the hens to make use of it to save them all the trial of the steps. Just a pull of the gate and a turn of the crank was all it would take. (He'd seen it in a movie.) Either hen could easily flap up to the handle, and their weight alone would lower the crank for a short ride to the second floor. But Uncle Henrietta only ever said, "I don't trust hot metal boxes with doors on 'em. Got a bad feeling about it. I once had a dream I roasted to a crisp in something like that."

So that was that.

Just outside the lobby, leaves swirled off the sidewalk onto the emerald-tiled entrance. People rushed past unaware, never noticing things like leaves or hens or hedgehogs. Most never stopped to look at the theater at all.

As he fixed a candy on his side that was threatening to slide off, Marcel watched a dark car slow and pull up in front of the theater.

"Hurry up! Dupree will be back soon," warned Uncle Henrietta. "We cut it too close the last time."

"Oh, Sister. You are a worrywart," said Auntie

Hen from somewhere behind the snack counter.

"There's always the elevator," Marcel suggested for the one hundred sixty-somethingish time. "Want me to summon it?"

"You know how I feel about it!" Uncle snapped back.

Marcel sighed. As the elevator *was* their one and only "Emergency Exit Plan" (he'd seen that in a movie too and thought it sounded like a good idea), he'd feel a lot better if they practiced it at least once.

It wouldn't be today.

Marcel followed Uncle to the grand staircase and noticed again the dark car puttering at the curb. The shadow of a man sat behind the wheel. He seemed to be waiting.

Marcel tripped over a snag in the carpet and caught himself. He was carrying mostly candy this morning, which was a lot heavier than popcorn. The Fruit Gems on his back only added to the load. The stairs would be trickier than normal.

They'd made it up only three steps when behind

them came a thump and a thrashing sound.

"Oh my, oh dear, oh, this is a problem!" came Auntie Hen's voice from behind the concession counter.

"Quit your fooling around and get out here!" ordered Uncle Henrietta.

"I would," came Auntie's muffled voice. "But I seem to be a little stuck!"

Uncle Henrietta stomped her foot. "Well, get unstuck!"

The thrashing continued. "I can't!"

Marcel set his armload of candy on the step and Uncle her paper sack of popcorn. Crossing the lobby, they made their way behind the glass counter stuffed with snacks. All appeared normal but for the sliding door on the back of the stand, off its track. The wide, feathered bottom of Auntie Hen was wiggling out the back, her skinny yellow legs and feet kicking wildly about.

"It was unlocked! We can have all the strawberry Gems we want!" clucked Auntie Hen.

Marcel tried the door. It didn't budge.

"Turn sideways!" said Uncle. "Suck in your feathers! If you didn't eat so many peppermints this morning, you'd slide right through!"

Auntie Hen's legs kept swinging.

"Grab a foot," Uncle said to Marcel. "I'll get the other."

They pulled. They pulled some more. The chicken didn't budge.

"We're running out of time," said a worried Uncle. She looked through the window of the concession stand to the entrance beyond. Marcel's eyes followed.

A little cloud of exhaust puffed in the far corner of the glass doors. Marcel couldn't see it now, but the dark car must still be there. What was it doing? He felt an uneasiness settle in his stomach.

(Or maybe he'd had a few too many peppermints too.)

Marcel thought hard. What might help Auntie slip through the door and fast? The soda machine didn't seem right. A slushie . . . ? Maybe.

No.

Butter. That slippery scrumptiousness generously pumped onto every awaiting popcorn tub.

He told Uncle Henrietta his idea.

"That's the worst plan I've ever heard!" she shouted. "Butter on a chicken? My gut's screaming it's a bad idea. But I don't see as we've got any choice!"

Marcel scrambled up the stack of heavy kernel sacks leaning against the back counter to the butter dispenser and threw a soda cup beneath it. He climbed onto the pump and jumped. Butter squirted out in great, greasy spurts. He jumped a bit more. Then he dropped the nearly full cup to a waiting Uncle Henrietta. Some splattered on her head.

"WORST THING I'VE EVER HEARD!" she squawked again.

As Marcel made his way down, he could see Auntie's coppery feathers grow slick as Uncle Henrietta poured the liquid butter over her backside. The grease would take ages to come out, he thought.

But she did smell delicious.

Uncle stopped pouring. "Grab a leg!" she ordered again, and she and Marcel pulled and twisted. Still the chicken didn't budge.

Just then there was a jangle at the doors. The three of them froze and looked up.

Gomer Dupree stood just outside, keys in hand.

A man in a dark suit stood beside him, his meaty fingers reaching for the handle.

CHAPTER 3

Hot Buttered Hen and Heartache

AUNTIE HEN SQUEEZED HER EYES SHUT. "I CAN'T look!" she squeaked.

Marcel's glasses slid off his face and dropped to the floor. "I can't see."

Uncle Henrietta groaned.

The men at the door stood talking. The shiny brass handle glinted under the man in the dark suit's grip, but the door, for now, remained closed. Gomer Dupree spoke excitedly, his hands turning like pinwheels.

Auntie Hen opened an eye. "What's he doing?" she asked.

"Does it matter?" Uncle clucked. "Pull!"

Marcel pulled with all his might, but his paws were slick. He slipped backward and went tumbling into the large spokes of the popcorn cart's bicycle-like wheels. He felt around for his spectacles, and finding them, threw them back on his nose.

Past the concession stand and beyond the glass doors, the men were arguing now. Gomer's keys flashed as he shook them. The man in the suit took his hand from the door handle and reached inside his jacket, where Marcel spotted . . . a *badge*. Marcel recognized it from all the action movies he'd seen, winking gold, like a shield. The sight of it gave him a dark feeling. Dark as dried-up Crystal Cola syrup.

The man pulled out a folded sheet of paper and began to paste it to the glass.

Gomer Dupree's shoulders drooped.

When the man in the suit finished smoothing out the paper and tacking down the edges, Marcel watched as Gomer shook his head miserably, shoved his keys back into the pocket of his overalls, and walked out of sight. The man in the suit followed.

"What's happening?" whispered Auntie Hen.

"How should I know?" answered Uncle Henrietta.

Something wasn't right. Marcel could feel it. Men with badges in the movies were always on some sort of official business and it was almost never good. Marcel shifted his feet. He nibbled his nails. The dark feeling felt sickly, ominously sweet.

He needed to know what was going on.

Marcel dropped to all fours and darted to the front doors, being sure to stick to the shadows in case the two men appeared again.

"Marcel!" squealed Auntie Hen.

"Get back here!" shouted Uncle.

Marcel ignored them. He had to find out where Gomer Dupree and the badge man had gone.

He slowed as he neared the glass and crept to the furthermost edge. He peeked out.

There they were on the sidewalk. Marcel watched as the men shook hands and the man in the suit climbed into the puttering car. This close, Marcel could see something stamped on the car's door.

Marcel was lucky he'd spent so many hours watching foreign films and movies for the hearing impaired. He'd taught himself to read using subtitles. "*Shirley River Building Inspector,*" he sounded out before the car pulled away from the curb.

A wilted Gomer Dupree watched the car drive off. When at last he looked away, the old Emerald City janitor walked across the street and disappeared inside a hardware store.

"What do you see?" came Auntie Hen's nervous squeak.

Marcel squinted up at the sheet of paper flapping on the door. The print was far too small to read from where he stood.

"It's the chicken pox, isn't it?" wailed Auntie. "Or the bird flu! I saw that in a movie. They put a sign on the door saying the place was contaminated with disease. We've contaminated the place, Uncle!"

"Hush, Sister!" snapped Uncle Henrietta. "Marcel. What do you see?"

There was no time to answer, for at that moment Gomer Dupree came shuffling out of the store with a large roll of paper under one arm and a plastic bag swinging from the other. He headed straight for Marcel, who scampered back behind the concession stand as fast as his short legs could carry him.

The three animals watched through the glass as Gomer pulled a writing utensil out of the bag and knelt on the paper. His arm swirled out a string of words. When he finished, he stood and taped the sign to the doors of the theater.

Gomer stepped back to admire his work. A strange look passed over his brown, wrinkled face. He slid off the cap covering his bald head and placed it over his heart. He stood that way for a full minute before shoving his cap back on and tramping away through the dry leaves on the pavement.

"This is all so puzzling," said Auntie Hen, still

wedged in the snack counter's sliding door. "What on earth is going on?"

"Darned if I know," answered her sister.

Marcel licked his lips. His heart still hammered in his chest. But as minutes ticked by, the hammering slowed and returned to its normal *thumpity-thump*.

An hour passed. At 11:30, a woman holding the hand of a little girl approached the doors. She stopped to take in the large sign Gomer Dupree had plastered to the front of the building, and the two walked away.

At 11:34, a tall man strode into the open, emerald-tiled vestibule, took one look, and strode off.

At 11:35, four elderly women with matching patent-leather pocketbooks shambled up to the glass. One pointed to the darkened ticket booth, another rifled through her purse for dollar bills. One tried to open the doors but found them locked. The last adjusted her bifocals and read from the poster. With glum looks, all four walked back in the direction they'd come.

It went on like this for the next half hour.

Eventually, the theatergoers dwindled. Then stopped.

Auntie Hen fell out of the candy counter with a *THWUNK*.

"Really?" said Uncle Henrietta. "You just fell out like that?"

"I get puffy when I'm anxious!"

Henrietta shook her head. "Honestly. Sometimes I don't know how we came from the same coop."

Marcel, his short spines still spotted with Fruit Gems, crept out from behind the stand. A beak latched on to his leg and pulled him back.

"We go together this time," said Uncle Henrietta.

They crossed the lobby. Auntie's buttery feathers gleamed under the crystal chandeliers. Uncle's too.

"Well, there's a sign there. Sure as there's butter on my backside. Now what?" asked Henrietta when they got to the doors.

Light shone through the paper; the dark words leapt off the page.

"I thought it might have pictures," said a disappointed Auntie Hen.

"I can read it," said Marcel. He cleared his throat and picked his way through the backward words. *"The Emerald City Theater is closed until further notice,"* he read. *"Thank you for all the years. Sincerely, Gomer Dupree, Owner."*

Auntie Hen gasped.

Uncle Henrietta moaned.

Marcel's face felt hot, and he swallowed hard.

Closed? What did that mean? Would they need to find a new place to live?

Marcel had grown used to the theater. Grown used to his popcorn-bucket house with the chewed door, nestled between the two hen sisters. To gathering armloads of candy every morning for breakfast—some might consider a candy breakfast a dream! He *liked* the smell of popcorn. It wasn't Dorothy's popcorn of course—Dorothy liked hers doused in butter with Parmesan cheese, in a pillow fort on the floor, and an old musical or *The Wizard of Oz* warbling away on the television. But for the past six months, the theater *had* been home.

He and the hens could get by on lime Fruit Gems for a while. Especially if they rationed them. But would they have enough food until the theater opened again? *If* it opened again? Would they need to find food elsewhere?

Would he have to go back out on the street?

Marcel's knees buckled.

"I need a hug," Auntie said.

"I need a Toffee Bean," said Uncle.

Marcel felt like he needed a nap. He promised himself that as soon as he returned to the torn, velvet cushion of seat 6HH and crawled inside his popcorn tub, he'd turn a few times, curl up, and pray for a sound, forgetful sleep.

But it would have to wait.

The hen sisters decided that since they'd already suffered a trip down the stairs, they might as well gather what food they could and save themselves the trial of another trip.

"Could stick all our goodies in that awful contraption and send it up," said Uncle, pointing to the small elevator. "You can handle it, can't you, Marcel?"

He couldn't. He couldn't fly up and reach the lever. But maybe an elevator full of sweets would be reason enough for the hens to try. . . .

He'd cross that bridge later.

As Auntie and Uncle raided what they could of the open concession stand and loaded it into the elevator, Marcel did another sweep of the theater. He was working hard at pulling over a cup of Chocolate Buttons he'd sniffed out when, suddenly, he heard a door open. Then voices.

Then the terrified squawks of the hen sisters and a thrashing of wings.

"He's got me! He's got me!" squealed Auntie Hen.

Marcel's stomach dropped like a stone.

He—Gomer Dupree—did not, in fact, have Auntie, though he was, at this very moment, chasing her down the theater aisle toward Marcel. Two others were hot on the tail feathers of Uncle Henrietta.

"You go that way!" shouted a bearded man to

Gomer. "Peterman, you go over there. We'll meet in the middle!"

"Marcel!" Auntie slipped through Gomer's grasp like a recently buttered hen. "Marcel! What do I do?" she squawked.

Uncle Henrietta flew at the bearded man's head and scratched at his shiny hard hat. "Get to safety, Hen!"

"Where?" she squealed.

Marcel couldn't breathe. His legs, he didn't think, would carry him.

If only they'd practiced his "Emergency Exit Plan."

"The elevator," he managed to spit out. "Get to the elevator and stop between floors! Stick to the plan!"

He sure hoped the hens remembered the plan.

Marcel sucked in his breath and sprang into action.

He hopped off the seat and ran down the row. He flew up the center aisle but turned four rows from the back to avoid a large boot. He could hear flapping wings, excited voices, and the near-constant squawking of the sisters. Marcel scrambled down the row to the end and waited, breathing hard.

He remembered a small hole in the wall on the other side of the theater, and he had a thought.

"Auntie! Uncle! Take the elevator! Don't wait for me! I'll lead them away! I've got a place to hide!" He could wait it out inside the hole until the men quit looking.

He just needed to make it there.

"I'm too scared!" Auntie squealed, as behind her, Gomer Dupree stumbled over Marcel's cup of Chocolate Buttons and they scattered like ants from a trampled anthill. The others were crawling down rows in pursuit of Uncle, who'd clambered under the seats.

Marcel's heart was a snare drum, and the blood pumping through his veins felt fizzy with soda pop. What they needed was a distraction.

All three men now crawled on the floor after

the hens. Each time any of them thought he'd caught one, the buttered hen would slip through his grasp. "Three on two!" one of the men shouted. "We corner them! Over there!"

Marcel planted his feet. He sucked up his courage. He waited for the men to crawl after the hens into the aisle.

Auntie emerged, then Uncle from under the seats ahead. Gomer appeared, then the others.

Marcel bolted. With every ounce of him, he made as much noise as his little lungs would allow. A hissing, howling ball of needles, Marcel made for the crawling men.

"Aaaaaaah!" shrieked one.

"Watch out!" barked the other.

"What *is* it?" Gomer cried. The men shuffled back, scrambling to their feet.

"The elevator!" Marcel shouted as he sailed past the hens. He chased the men toward the front of the theater as the hens raced out the back.

Just as a growling, spluttering Marcel cornered

the three, Marcel heard the rattle of the elevator gate. The freight elevator knocked and rumbled to life.

The hens were escaping!

Suddenly the look in the men's eyes went from shock to determination.

Marcel gulped.

He whirled around and tore up the aisle. He wove through seats, down rows, banked off walls, trying to shake off his pursuers. He spotted the hole in the wall and ran faster.

He was just a few steps from freedom, when suddenly . . .

FOOMP.

Everything went black.

Marcel felt himself tumbling around in the darkness.

"I got it, Peterman!" he heard a voice above him shout. "I'm taking it to the truck! You find the chickens!"

"They disappeared!"

"Keep looking! Meet me back at the office!" the voice barked.

Marcel rattled around in what he now recognized to be some sort of wooden crate. The man jogged up the aisle. Cool, autumn air shot through the box's cracks as they slammed through the front doors. There was a sailing sensation as Marcel's box was pitched into the bed of the truck.

(At least that's where Marcel assumed he'd crashed.)

He heard a truck door open and slam.

He heard an engine rumble to life and felt the ground beneath him vibrate.

He knew, as the sharp air began to sweep violently through the cracks and into a small knothole in the side of the crate, that he was rushing away from the Emerald City Theater.

And try as he might to ignore it, something told him . . .

He was farther now from Dorothy than he'd ever been before.

CHAPTER 4

(Not) Kansas

THE TRUCK BUMPED DOWN THE STREET, SLOWLY and haltingly at first, then with lengthening patches of speed. It fairly flew now, the miles stretching out like saltwater taffy.

Marcel put an eye up to the hole in the box. His line of vision wasn't good. He could see only a tool chest and several large buckets of paint. One bucket rolled on its side, spilling yellow paint into the truck bed.

Marcel thought hard. He could try to chew his way out, but then what? Jump from the racing truck? Hide in a toolbox and hope he wouldn't be found? Might the truck return to the theater eventually? If Marcel could just get back, back to the hen sisters, who were probably waiting for him in the elevator or hiding in the air shaft this very minute, everything would be okay.

Hiding seemed like the best plan.

Marcel scrambled up on his hind legs and was about to get to work, when he saw something move out of the corner of his eye. He dropped back down and went over to get a better look.

Fruit Gems littered the box. Some had fallen from Marcel's spines in the kerfuffle. But there on the ground in the middle of the box lay a small cocoon. It must have been secured somewhere inside and come loose. Marcel lifted it carefully and cradled it in his paws. He could feel something very alive inside.

He tried to make his voice as soothing as could be. "Are you okay?" he whispered.

The cocoon lay still, listening.

Marcel looked around but found nothing that might keep the creature from sliding about. The threads that had held it in a cozy corner were shredded and torn.

Marcel felt terrible. If he hadn't barged in to the cocoon's house . . .

"I can hold on to you, if you'd like. You'd be safer that way. Would you like that?" he asked, waiting a moment to see what the cocoon would do.

It wiggled.

Marcel thought it looked like an affirmative wiggle. "Well, good then"—he thought a moment—"*Toto*. Yes, I'll call you Toto." He patted the cocoon gently, and a small smile crept over his face.

He wasn't alone. The thought instantly soothed him a little.

Marcel gnawed at the wood until his gums were sore. He hadn't gotten very far on the hole, when suddenly, with a jolt, the truck skidded to a stop.

The box flew to the front and thumped against the cab. Marcel thumped around too, but he managed to hold the cocoon close to him protectively. He cocked his ears and listened.

A blue jay jeered at something in the distance.

There was a rustling of dried reeds.

He heard the truck door open, heavy boots hit the ground, the crunch of gravel under footsteps.

The tailgate *thunk*ed open.

"Seen a lot of things in my day," came a voice. "But chickens living in a theater and a porcupine . . ."

Marcel frowned. He wasn't a porcupine. He was small. Dorothy's pet. He'd helped Gomer keep the theater clean. He was no wild animal.

"Well, that just about takes the cake!"

The wooden box, with Marcel inside, was snatched up.

He tumbled around as they bumped along. He tried to brace himself in one corner but rolled to the next. Fruit Gems slid back and forth along the floor. Marcel clutched Toto with one arm.

Sunlight filtered in, flashing, then dimming in the shadows. Heavy footfalls crashed through what Marcel guessed were grasses and reeds. The spicy scent of autumn leaves pummeled his nose.

A boot splashed through a puddle, and the

thwock of mud sounded, for all the world, like a threat. The boots stopped.

The box hovered. Light glinted off Marcel's spectacles, which had fallen off and lay close by. The blue jay cried.

The man with the box breathed in deeply. "Smell that fresh air!" He gave the box a little shake, and Marcel rolled into a ball, clutching Toto to him for safekeeping. The cocoon seemed to curl up and thank him. Marcel waited, not daring to move.

"Don't know how you got in the Emerald City," said the man, and Marcel felt the box being placed on the ground. "But you sure as shootin' aren't getting back!"

A boot crashed into the box's side.

Marcel pitched and slammed into the wood, followed by several Fruit Gems. He flopped about mercilessly as the box tumbled down a hill.

The box caught air and time slowed. Marcel squeezed his eyes shut. He wasn't fond of bruises or broken bits. He quickly prayed for a painless death, to wake up somewhere over the rainbow. He braced for impact. The box was falling. *He* was falling.

BOOM!

Silence.

Silence.

Not the cheep of a sparrow. Not the rustle of switchgrass. Not a single moan or sigh of the wind.

Silence.

Was he *dead?* Marcel opened an eye.

He must be dead. Things were fuzzy. He was leaving his body for hedgehog heaven.

He was surprised how very real it all felt and how clear his thinking was. He expected more . . . fanfare. And possibly music.

Something wiggled in his arms.

Toto! Poor Toto was dead too! He'd gotten the poor thing caught in his dramatic final exit.

(He had to admit it was an exit fit for the movies, though.)

Just then, a strawberry Fruit Gem wedged in a crack in the ceiling came loose, clunked Marcel in the head, and fell to the floor. Marcel blinked at it.

Wait, was he *not* dead?

Marcel spotted the fuzzy shape of his glasses nearby and scrambled over to grab them. He put them on.

A large crack split one lens and one of the arms was bent, and his poor glasses fell off his nose. Marcel worked at the arm until it was marginally better. The spectacles mostly stayed put now, but there was nothing to be done about the cracked lens. He looked around.

The box, strewn with Fruit Gems, was mangled and broken. Dust clouded in from a large hole and glinted in the light. Marcel popped his head out.

All around was patchy brown grass.

And that was about it.

He needed to get out. And now that he wasn't dead, he needed to find that truck.

Marcel gathered his courage, and with Toto in his arms, he sucked in his stomach, pinched his eyes shut, and flopped out into the light.

Marcel rolled and came to a stop in a hollow in the dirt.

All was grass. It waved along the hill and sprang up in patches of green and brown, yellows and burgundies all around. He recognized wildflowers, too.

The theater had played a lovely documentary on wildflowers once.

Spires of goldenrod. White sweet clover. Purply blue chicory, shaped like sunshine, and the spiny leaves and wilted white blooms of mountain mint that had scented the air with delicious breezes not so long ago. And between all this blooming bounty, there were rocks of every size, a potato bug, a little house with a flat, mushroom roof and winding, dusty trails, and . . .

A house with a mushroom roof?

Marcel took off his glasses, rubbed them against the fur on his belly, and put them back on. He blinked.

Not just one house, but many. Mushroom houses. Houses in the crooks of stones with leafy awnings. A few rusted soup cans lying on their sides, labels faded and pulling away, lids peeled back, pebbles lining the walk. There was even a glass milk bottle covered in moss.

Marcel heard the door of the truck slam and the rev of an engine. His stomach flip-flopped, and he whirled about, trying to find the direction it came from, somewhere up the hill.

Auntie Hen. Uncle Henrietta. The theater . . .

Dorothy.

Tires peeled out on the gravel road. It wasn't long before the growl of the truck was a silent ache in his ears. Marcel's throat tightened and he blinked away hot tears. He swallowed.

The truck was gone. He was here. He was lost. *Lost* lost.

No. No, he just needed to figure out *where* he was and what he was going to do about it. This wasn't like before, he told himself. He'd found his way to the theater once. Surely he could do it again. He had a good nose. And the smell of a hundred years of popcorn is strong.

Marcel looked down at Toto. "Don't be scared. I—I'll figure out something," he said.

The cocoon shivered.

Suddenly, something whizzed past his left ear.

It flew straight into the box and drove itself into a lime Fruit Gem stuck to the side. Marcel turned in time to see the Gem fall to the ground, a sharp pebble sunk deep in its flesh.

"Toto?" Marcel said in a high whisper. "I have a feeling we're not in Kansas anymore."

CHAPTER 5

Marcel Meets a Moth (and More) in Mousekinland

MARCEL SCRAMBLED BACK TO THE BOX QUICK as a wink and dove inside. He hid in the darkest corner and tucked Toto safely under his arm, away from enemy fire.

What was after him? What should he do?

Dorothy wouldn't shrink back. She'd face whatever was out there. She's brave and heroic and never rolls up in a ball and shakes with fright.

Marcel didn't know why these thoughts came to his mind then, but then again, there was no telling when the memories would come.

Dorothy *was* brave. She was the first person to

ever touch Marcel without fear of being pricked by one of his quills. And oh, she had been pricked.

Twenty-seven times to be exact.

He remembered her reaching into the cage the first time she saw him at the shelter. Marcel had rolled into a ball and chittered. He was scared and very tired of all the pokes and prods of curious fingers. Tired of moving from place to place and person to person. The stress of it all had been too much.

First there was the pet store, then Sweetie's. But Sweetie Jones met a guy. So she shipped Marcel off to Ed's. Ed liked Marcel's spines—thought they were "killer." But he got mad when Marcel got scared and the quills came out. Darla Pickens had been allergic; Marty Henkle got a cat. He was passed around several more owners, never for very long, until the last had brought him to the shelter and left. There, people, lots of them, with their poke-y, prod-y fingers, came by regularly. People looking to take him home.

No one ever did.

And then there was a girl.

"I know what it's like," she'd whispered. "I didn't get to stay in my first home either. I've been moved around too. But I'll take care of you if you'll trust me. Trust—it only takes a little."

But all Marcel knew then was that the world was too harsh and people unkind.

Also, they were fickle.

He'd rolled into a ball and jumped when she'd tried to pet him. He'd drawn a pinprick of blood.

She brought him straight home.

Dorothy.

His Dorothy.

It didn't happen suddenly, but in time she peeled back a corner of his bruised and timid heart and climbed inside.

After a few dozen Band-Aids, that is.

Dorothy—*his* Dorothy—was fearless. Marcel was not.

He needed another plan.

The late-afternoon sun shone into the box and lit the two strawberry Fruit Gems slumped in the corner. They gleamed like rubies.

Rubies!

Maybe it was all the times he's seen it happen just like this, but instinctively, he laid Toto down and grabbed the Fruit Gem closest to him—a lime—and measured it against his foot.

He'd put the red Gems on his feet. He'd close his eyes and click his candy heels. With each click, he'd recite these words: There's no place like home. There's no place like—

Marcel stopped.

Had he lost his mind? Ruby slippers? This wasn't *The Wizard of Oz. The Wizard of Oz* was a movie. Magic happened in movies. It did *not* happen in real life.

Marcel looked up from the green candy clutched in his paws. Through a hairline crack in the box, an eyeball peered at him.

Marcel screamed. Something else screamed. A patter of feet flew off into the weeds. Marcel grabbed Toto, crept up to the crack, and peeked out.

Grass. There was nothing but swaying grass.

"Hello," said a voice behind him.

Marcel screeched and rolled into a ball.

"Oh, I've frightened you!" The voice was kind, soft, like velvet. "I'm sorry. How rude of me. Frightening a hero like that . . ."

A . . . *hero?* Marcel opened an eye.

Two feathery yellow antennae poked into the box, followed by furred feet and legs a deep rusty color. A downy white head with two dark eyes came next, and then two great wings of a green so enchanting the hedgehog's breath caught. The wings unfolded, and the evening sun, low in its descent, shone through them. They glowed like green starlight.

Before Marcel stood a moth. The largest moth he'd ever seen.

"I'm Oona," said the moth. "And you are?"

"M-marcel." His name slopped out. He found himself raising the cocoon in his paws. "And this is Toto."

"How do you do? I'm so glad"—she paused, and Marcel thought he noticed her wince a little—

"so glad we bumped into each other." She looked behind her and smiled. "It looks like there are others here who'd like to greet you too."

"Are you a witch?" The question tumbled out, and Marcel regretted it immediately. Clearly he'd watched the movie a few too many times, and possibly he was suffering from a bump on the head, but glowing there like she was, all he could think about was Glinda.

Glinda the Good Witch, who got Dorothy Gale home.

The moth let out a jolly laugh. "No, not a witch," she answered. "But from what I've heard, they might say you've done away with one. Come and see." Oona crept backward, out of the box.

Marcel scrambled to the hole, and into the light he came. Into the grasses and wildflowers. Back to the miniature houses scattered prettily about.

"Look here," said Oona.

Marcel turned to face Oona, who was pointing a furred leg near the bottom of Marcel's wooden box.

Marcel gasped.

In a tangle of crushed grass lay the end of a thick, serpentine tail. It was scaled and striped red, black, and white. It lay very still. Marcel felt a shiver go through him. He tried to keep himself from curling up.

"Don't be afraid," Oona told him. "She can't hurt you now."

Oona stretched her wings and floated to a rock overlooking the tiny village. "Come out, come out!" she sang. "Come, Mousekins! It's okay! Come see what this visitor has done!"

From behind every rock, from inside tin cans and mushroom huts, between reeds and out of the prickly green bellies of a few milkweed pods waving in the evening breeze, popped ears, whiskers, tiny pink noses, and tails. First twenty, then fifty, then hundreds of brown field mice filled Marcel's view.

A plump mouse with an acorn-cap hat came forward. He took off his hat and bowed. "I, Mayor Mortodellus Mousekin, would like to thank you for your service and welcome you to Mousekinland."

Marcel pinched himself. He blinked a few times and rubbed a hand over his eyes.

Was he dreaming? This couldn't be real, could it? It was too alike.

His flying box had landed in *Mouse*kinland? Had it any relation to *Munchkin*land?

He must be dreaming, Marcel decided. Or he was dead.

Yes, probably dead.

Just then, a tiny pebble shot out from behind a milkweed pod and *thunk!* It lodged itself in a Fruit Gem a small mouse was attempting to sneak away. The mouse squeaked and ran off.

Marcel watched as Mayor Mousekin's face grew pink. Then red. He turned around. The rest of the village followed suit.

"Scarlet Mousekin, put that sling-shooter away this instant!" he bellowed.

A pair of tiny ears and a little whiskered face popped out from behind the belly of the milkweed pod. The face frowned.

"But, Papa!"

"Not a word!" shouted the mouse mayor. "Not a single word. Get down from there this instant and greet our guest."

"But those—"

"Nope, *nein, nyet*!"

"But—"

"Enough!" The mayor threw down his acorn cap. "No daughter of mine will behave like a common varmint! Get ahold of yourself, girl!" He turned back to Marcel with an embarrassed smile. The sea of villagers did the same. "My apologies. My daughter—she's young and, well, opinionated. Gets ideas in her head . . . you understand."

Marcel didn't, but he nodded anyway.

"You'll stay the night, won't you? As our esteemed guest?" He pointed to the striped tail snaking out from under Marcel's box. "She's prowled the east field ever since she found us here. We owe you a debt of thanks." He turned to face the village, grabbed Marcel's free hand, and held it high.

"I hereby declare a holiday! A night off is certainly deserved, and we have reason to celebrate! The milk snake is dead!"

At these words, the village erupted in cheers. Caps spun dizzily into the air. Tiny mouselings drooled at the prospect of roasted seeds and berry tarts.

Marcel cleared his throat. "I do need to be getting back," he tried to tell the mayor, thinking of his theater, the hens. But the ruckus drowned him out.

Scrambling up to her father's side, the little mouse from the milkweed pod narrowed her eyes at Marcel. Marcel shielded Toto as best he could.

As the cheering of Mousekins died, Marcel tried again. "Auntie Hen and Uncle Henrietta will be worried," he told the mayor.

"Tomorrow, tomorrow. There will be plenty of time for that tomorrow," assured Mayor Mousekin. And as he said this, he plucked his daughter's sling-shooter out of her hands and stashed it under his cap. "Off to bed with you now, Scarlet," he told the mouse. "It's getting late and we can't be too careful. There will be other parties."

It was the little mouse's turn to flush an angry red. She stomped off.

But not before shooting Marcel a venomous look.

"We'll get you on your way tomorrow," the mayor repeated before turning to leave. "No doubt about it."

The sun began to slip, taking the light slowly with it, and Marcel was left standing there as the whole village scattered before him. The green moth floated down beside him. He felt a sort of comfort as he watched Oona's wings open and close. It was like watching a flower bloom.

Ruby slippers wouldn't help, but maybe this moth could, he thought.

(Magic was a nice idea, but it certainly wasn't practical.)

"Do *you* think you could help me?" he asked. "Help me get back to the hens? I need to get back as soon as possible."

Oona rested a small, furred foot on his paw.

"Not so fast. It's almost dark, and there are far worse things out there in the dark than you can see now in the light. Eat. Get some rest. I suspect you have a long journey . . . ahead?"

At her words, Marcel felt his head throb. His legs, which had held up so well during the strain of the day, wobbled. His eyelids felt heavy.

A *journey* was not what he wanted to hear.

A long journey was the *last* thing he wanted to hear.

As all of Mousekinland bustled about, gathering food and making preparations for a night of merriment, Oona leaned close.

"Rest now," she said. "Tomorrow you begin."

CHAPTER 6

Scarecrow

MORNING DAWNED WITH ORANGE SKIES AND birdsong, and Mousekinland was abuzz. The last days of autumn were upon them. Winter was drawing near. Since their latest move, the whole town had been well behind schedule. Days, nights—it didn't matter. There was work to do.

Mice, young and old, scurried by. One with a seed caught in its teeth, another pulling a cart full of acorns. A school of youngsters shouldered leafy packs stuffed with the last wrinkled blackberries of fall.

A round mouse with big eyes and a scruffy look, trying to catch up to his classmates, dropped a berry from his pack. It rolled down a short hill into Marcel's borrowed burrow and bopped him on the nose, startling him out of his sleepy daze.

Marcel blinked a few times. He rubbed the sleep from his eyes. He sighed deeply.

The night before had been a carnival of feasting and dancing—grass pipes and reedy flutes singing; laughing fiddles, strung with silk spiderwebs, *twing*ing. Mushroom-cap drums had thumped into the air, while the sparks of tiny fires lifted to join the stars. The smell of roasted acorns, marsh onions, and the sweet scent of apples warming on stones curled deliciously into the night.

And Marcel, longing for the safety of his popcorn-tub house, had watched into the wee hours, his thoughts turning again and again to a different night.

One with dark trees. Screeching birds. The wind wailing like the Wicked Witch. The first of many nights he'd spent in the wild, very lost and far from home. The night he'd lost her. *Dorothy*.

But the boy, he reminded himself. *The boy, the bird, the bicycle basket, the basset hound.*

They were proof it never could've been different.

Marcel took a deep breath, put on his cracked spectacles, and went over the prior day's events.

Leaving the theater. His box. The milk snake. Oona and Mousekinland.

A journey. He sighed again.

He'd best get to it.

Marcel grabbed Toto and, finding a small cart nearby, he loaded his Fruit Gems and headed toward the smell of breakfast—past a troop of mice hoarding corn kernels in a rotting log; past a group huddled over a long Mousekinland table with tiny needles and thread, sewing sumac leaves into blankets; past others stacking honeycomb in wobbly towers.

In the center of town on a rocky platform, the mayor orchestrated the harvest symphony. His eyes fell on Marcel and he scrambled down.

"Aha! And how were your accommodations? Comfortable, I hope! Yes, well, it must have been. Looks like you've slept the day away."

Marcel looked to the sun just now creeping over the horizon and wondered how long the mice of Mousekinland had been up. "It was very comfortable. Thank you," he replied. "The grass was . . . soft."

"Good, good. We do pride ourselves on our hospitable lodgings."

Marcel looked around. The field positively fluttered with activity, but nowhere did he see the green moth. "Where's Oona?"

"Oona?" said the mayor absentmindedly. His eyes followed a small band of mouselings rolling a bruised apple toward a hole in the ground. One mouse, happily chomping on a clover leaf, pushed with a single claw.

The mayor clapped his paws sharply, and the youngster nearly leapt out of his fur. Mayor Mousekin gave him a stern look before turning back to Marcel. "Now, then? Oh yes. Oona. The moth, yes? I say, we only met her just yesterday. Couldn't tell you where she flew off to."

"But . . ." Marcel felt his heart beat a little faster, a bead of sweat gathered on his brow.

In *The Wizard of Oz* it was the wise and beautiful Glinda who told Dorothy Gale to follow the yellow brick road, Glinda who helped her get back to Kansas—home. Marcel wasn't expecting magic after his conversation with Oona, of course, but he trusted her somehow. He would've liked to ask her for directions at least.

"I—I thought she'd help me get back to the theater," he stammered.

"The theater?" The mayor frowned. "Just go back the way you came. That's what we mice do when we've ventured off. Just sniff around a bit. The nose picks up all sorts of clues."

Marcel clutched Toto a little tighter. "But I came a long way. In a truck! I didn't leave a trail to sniff." His voice wavered a little and he tried to steady it.

"Hmm. That is a problem," said the mayor,

scratching his chin. "Wish we could be of assistance. But we're in our busiest season, you know, and trying to make up for lost time."

"But you said—"

"Take what you need—food, supplies. Or not. You're welcome to stay here too, of course." The mayor went on. "Nothing wrong with picking up and putting down roots elsewhere when times get tough."

Just then a loud *CRACK* echoed through the air. A wave of corn kernels spilled from the log, and the mayor squeaked in shocked alarm. "You'll forgive me!" he shouted to Marcel as he scrambled off his platform. "We've got a leak! This'll set us back days!"

"Can I help?" Marcel called after him. But the mayor waved him off.

"No, no, we've got our systems!"

Marcel watched as the mayor joined the rest of Mousekinland rushing to the log, gathering kernels by hand and working to save their winter stores. He bit his lip as he looked down at Toto and patted the little cocoon. It wriggled contentedly.

"I guess we're on our own," he said quietly.

(He tried hard to sound assuring.)

Marcel found a cart piled high with leaf sacks and selected one off the top. He stuffed his Fruit Gems inside and threw it over his shoulder. He took another sack and tore a corner away to make a pouch for Toto and settled the cocoon snuggly inside. He strapped that on too. The pouch fit close to his furry heart. Marcel looked down at Toto and bit his lip. His legs felt heavy already.

But not as heavy as his heart did.

"Psst!"

Marcel looked up and squinted.

"Psst!"

Marcel turned. An eyeball appeared between two blades of grass.

"Follow the yellow stink-water!" said a familiar-sounding voice. It tinkled like a broken bell.

"Follow the—"

"Follow the—just get to the road! Up the hill!" it ordered. The blades of grass popped back into place, and a rustle was heard through the grasses beyond.

Marcel looked back at the village of Mousekinland. Mice scurried frantically from marsh to mushroom, knot to knoll, from leaf to log, the whole town employed with the important work of salvaging their harvest.

Maybe he should wait and talk to the mayor again. Maybe one of the mice had traveled to the city and could give him a map.

Marcel turned back to where the voice had disappeared.

But the hens, he thought to himself. Had they returned to the balcony? Were they hiding in the air shaft? Now that he thought about it, it wasn't hard to imagine the two sisters still stuck in the elevator with the enormous pile of candy they'd managed to collect that day. If Marcel didn't return soon, who knows how many Cinnamon Snaps Auntie would stuff herself with.

It wouldn't be the first time she'd made herself sick. . . .

And Uncle Henrietta always had a bad feeling about that metal box. . . .

There wasn't time to wait, Marcel decided.

He'd gamble on the voice.

The farther Marcel got from Mousekinland, the quieter it became. *Up the hill*, the voice had said. As he climbed, all was the shushing of grass and the distant honking of geese. He found the trace of a matted path and followed it. The road was near. He could smell the rubber tires and motor oil of days gone by. But where exactly had that voice run off to?

Marcel came to the roadside. The packed dirt and gravel ran as far as the eye could see, and was buttressed by fields and roofed by a pale-blue sky. For miles, nothing stirred. There wasn't a car to be seen, not a truck to be heard. This was a lonely country road.

Marcel steadied his glasses, secured his pack, and stepped out of the grass slowly, carefully. Toto stirred against his chest.

The voice had said something about stink-water,

hadn't it? *Yellow* stink-water. The only yellow in sight was a patch of goldenrod. It waved at him.

Marcel trotted a few yards to the left. He turned and went a few steps to the right. "Hello?" he called. "Hello? Are you there?"

There was no sign of the voice.

"What do you think, Toto?" he asked the cocoon. "Right or left?"

Marcel waited, hoping Toto might signal to him in some itty-bitty way, and held his breath. He didn't want to miss it.

But the warm cocoon was still. Toto must have fallen asleep.

Just sniff around a bit, the mayor had said, and Marcel could think of nothing else but to take this advice, so he sniffed for any hints.

Sniff. The tang of dried grass.

Sniff. The fading perfume of a few dying daisies and goldenrod.

Sniff. Sunshine, clean and musky.

Sniff. And the Fruit Gems in his pack. His stomach rumbled.

Maybe a snack would help.

Marcel pulled the pack from his shoulder, shoved a hand inside, and was about to pull out a Gem, when a tiny voice sounded high above him.

"Don't even think about it," it said.

On the side of the road, atop a leaning wooden fence post and gold with sun, stood the small mouse from yesterday. She wore a walnut-shell shield of sorts strapped to her chest. A green leaf-cape slipped down her back, and her old sling-shooter was tucked in a belt made of braided weeds. A sack of sharp pebbles dangled from her belt.

Bony arms thrust out at angles and hands on her hips, she looked like a tiny scarecrow standing over the field. She glared at him and crossed her arms.

"Oh," said Marcel. "It's you. Hello again."

The tiny mouse ignored him. She slid down a broken piece of fence and landed nearby. She thrust out an open paw. "Hand them over," she demanded.

Marcel stepped back. "Hand what over?"

Her frown deepened. "You know what. Those awful gooey fruits you got." She moved her paw closer.

Marcel clutched the leaf-pack tighter. "But they're—"

"But nothing," the mouse interrupted, stomping over and grabbing the sack out of Marcel's paws.

Marcel looked down at her. She wasn't bigger than four pieces of popcorn stacked one on top of the other. He swallowed.

She threw the sack down in front of her, and it burst open like a treasure chest. The Gems gleamed.

"Nobody listens to the smallest mouse. Everybody thinks they know better," she griped, bending over and taking a strawberry Fruit Gem in each paw.

Marcel cleared his throat lightly. "But what do you want them for?"

"For this."

Marcel watched as the little mouse tossed the Gems over her shoulder, where they bounced off a bit of fencing, sailed through the air, and with two definitive *plops*, disappeared into a puddle. Marcel swallowed again.

"You can't just traipse into the east field with weird new fruits and not expect someone to come sniffing around. It's highly dangerous! And that color! That *green*! Soon as I saw it, I knew you needed help. It's downright unnatural! We got eagles in these parts, you know!" The mouse kicked away the remaining Gems, snatched up the empty sack and shoved it in Marcel's direction. "Nobody ever listens to the smallest mouse, but I'll show them. Here!"

Marcel took the sack from her microscopic paw. "I'm sorry," he said. "I didn't know."

"Of course you didn't know! But I do!" she cried. She turned then and began marching down the middle of the road. Marcel followed . . .

But only after he'd gone and saved as many Gems as he could and stuffed them back in his pack, careful to keep any unnatural colors out of sight.

He wasn't about to throw away his only snack. He'd been hungry before.

Marcel looked in the sack.

Limes again. He sighed. *Always limes.*

Marcel caught up to the mouse, who was in the middle of some sort of speech.

". . . It's like I always say. You can't just run every time." She patted her sling-shooter. "You gotta carry some weapons! Nobody has any defensive instincts around here, and they think I'm the one who's lost her mind. Always keeping me cooped up. Never letting me do anything! Saying I'm accident prone!" She trailed off a little. "Well, there was that thing with the fire, but that wasn't my fault. I've got ideas! I'll show them!" She turned quickly, narrowed her eyes at Marcel, and pointed the tiniest claw in Marcel's direction. "And *you're* going to help me!"

"I am?" he answered.

She nodded. "Yup! Come on, prickly thing. I'm gonna get you home. I'll prove to him I know a thing or two about a thing or two. I'm brave, and I can take care of myself! And you!" She began to stomp down the road. "We're gonna work together. Like a trade!"

"You're going to help me get back to the theater?" Marcel felt his chest fill. A hard lump caught in his throat.

"Oh, sure!" The little mouse turned around, took one look at him, and rolled her eyes. "It's not like it's a big deal. Everyone's always taking expeditions for this or that. It's what we mice do. And anyway, it's my chance to show 'em what I'm made of."

"All by yourself?"

Marcel watched as the mouse opened her mouth. He thought he saw one eye twitch ever so slightly.

"Yea—yeah," she stammered at last. "Of course by myself! I do it all the time."

"And your father said it was okay?"

A crease lodged itself in the mouse's forehead. "Enough with the questions, you overgrown thistle. I know what I'm doing, and it's all just fine. Don't you worry your prickly little head about it."

"All right. If you say so," said Marcel. "But can I ask one more question?"

"No."

Maybe not a question, then. But introductions were important.

Marcel took a step forward and gestured to the sack strapped to his chest. "This—this is Toto. And I'm Marcel. I'm very pleased to make your acquaintance. Your name's Scarlet, isn't it?"

She huffed. "That depends," she said gruffly. "My *father* calls me Scarlet, but everyone *else* calls me Scamp."

"Why don't they call you Scarlet?"

The mouse didn't hesitate. She whipped the shooter from her belt, snatched a pebble, flung it inside the pocket of the sling, and fired it into the air. It sailed off and disappeared into the bright-orange leaves of a nearby tree.

A loud *caw!* cracked the air, and a large black crow flew up and away toward a line of trees in the distance, complaining as it went.

"I didn't hurt him," said Scamp. "Just gave him a good scare."

"Wow," said Marcel. It was like something from a movie.

"Crows eat mice, you know." She holstered her sling-shooter and straightened her shoulders. "They call me *Scamp* because I'm wily. You don't want to mess with me."

"Scamp. I . . ." Marcel wanted to ask one more time if she was doubly sure it was okay with her father that she join him, but from the look on the mouse's face, he knew there'd be trouble to pay. "I—I'm glad to have you along, Scamp." Awkwardly, he put out a sweaty paw to shake.

(She made him a little nervous.)

Scamp gave Marcel's paw one firm pump. "Charmed," she said. She noticed, then, Marcel's bulging leaf-sack. "Heyyy . . . what's in there? You didn't—"

"What, th-this?" Marcel stammered, feeling his face grow hot.

The Fruit Gems had to stay secret; he had a few

ideas about what they might be good for. Marcel lied. "Rocks!" he said, a little too loud. "It's filled with rocks. It's good for, uh . . . the muscles!"

Scamp looked dubious.

"And, um, weaponry and such! Ammunition!" Marcel cleared his throat and changed the subject. "Well, uh, what's next?" he asked, peering off at the road rushing in opposite directions.

Scamp still looked doubtful, but she pointed north. "Up ahead. The yellow stink-water."

"Oh, yes."

Scamp trotted a few paces and knelt down. "There. See that? It's stink-water. It came from your truck."

Marcel inspected it. He sniffed.

Paint! It was the yellow paint that had spilled in the truck bed! And sure enough, golden drips and drabs leapt out from the dusty road as far as the eye could see.

"If we follow it, it should lead you back to that truck," said the mouse.

A sharp cry sounded high overhead.

Marcel rolled up in a ball. Scamp ducked and expertly pulled her cape and shield over her head to hide. Her nose peeked out of the hood, and she searched the sky with two sparkling black eyes.

There was nothing but miles of blue and a few wispy clouds.

"We keep one eye on the sky and the other on the road. And we stop at night. Come on," said Scamp.

Marcel followed obediently, and with each drop of stink-water paint they passed, he felt his heart grow lighter.

It wasn't ruby slippers or a flying balloon like the Wizard of Oz had, but a trail? A yellow stink-water road?

It sounded just as good.

CHAPTER 7

Nose and Noggin

SPLASH AFTER SPLASH, SPLATTER AFTER SPLOTCH, Marcel and Scamp followed the stink-water road as the sun climbed higher.

They continued as the sun lingered for lunch. (Marcel and Scamp lingered over a few berries they'd found growing on a bush next to the road, suffering several thorns in the process.)

They followed the trail long after the sun had sunk low in the sky.

And with every drop of paint, Marcel found himself remembering. He couldn't help it.

The last time he'd done anything close to

following a trail like this was a few days after Dorothy had brought him home.

He remembered her opening his cage. She'd thought it would cheer him up to explore a bit. "Go ahead," she'd said. "My home is yours now."

Wary, he'd hidden deep under the bureau by the stairs, where she couldn't reach him. Dorothy had lain on her stomach for hours trying to coax him out.

"Come on, Marcel," she'd pleaded. "You're safe here. Just come out. I won't hurt you."

There are a lot of ways to get hurt, he wanted to tell her. *I'm not so worried about a bump or a bruise*. And he remembered noticing for the first time how brown her eyes were. Brown with flecks of gold.

Those eyes kept pleading. "Come on," she'd said. "Where's your courage? It only takes a little, you know."

Instead, he shook and chittered at her. Every time she slipped her hand under the bureau, he'd jump so that his quills grazed her fingertips, and she'd pull her hand away in pain. It was like a dance. Him quaking. Her following his every move. He was never coming out from under there. *Never*.

It was a trail of gingersnap crumbs that changed his mind.

Sometimes a trail is all it takes to lead you home.

It was like that with her. Dorothy always had a way of knowing just what he liked. Not bugs and mealworms like other hedgehogs. It just so happened that all his favorite things were her favorites too. Snacks in general, but gingersnaps, popcorn, banana slices with a swipe of peanut butter, scrambled eggs with hot dogs . . .

Show tunes and old movies.

Bubble baths and fuzzy blankets.

The smell of lavender fabric softener.

It was like they were made for each other.

And maybe they were. For a little while anyway.

It didn't matter. Maybe he and Dorothy *were* made for each other, but that was the past. That one decision more than six months ago now had changed everything.

The boy. It all started with that boy—Ethan.

The boy, the bird, the bicycle basket, the basset hound.

"Most mice think the nose is the only true way to sniff out food or danger, but oh no," Scamp was shouting from up ahead.

Marcel's memories hitched themselves to a cloud and floated away.

"Noses aren't the only thing! Not at all," said Scamp. "You gotta use your instincts, your noggin! That's how I found this stink-water trail here. I knew there had to be a clue to get you back. A good sniffer isn't the only badge of honor a mouse has. And keeping out of trouble isn't always the best thing, I always say!"

Scamp did talk a lot, Marcel thought. From the moment they started out, she seemed to stuff every available minute with words—well, excepting the time Marcel had inquired about a charred field of soybeans they'd passed. "Mind your business," she'd said simply. "It wasn't my fault."

The mouse stopped walking now to let Marcel

catch up. She grabbed a pebble and aimed her sling-shooter at the dried-up carcass of a cicada a few yards away. When the pebble hit, it exploded into a puff of dust. "Yep. Trouble comes looking for *you*. It's best to be prepared, carry a weapon. I need a sword."

"Do you think we should stop for a rest?" Marcel asked when he reached her. His feet were sore from the sharp grit of the road, and he'd been lagging behind the last hour. His stomach growled angrily.

But Scamp started moving again, a kick in her step. "It's at least an hour before dark. We'll stop then. It's safer to travel during the day."

They were going uphill now, huffing and puffing and choking on the dust of the road. The hill crested a way off, the road disappearing somewhere beyond.

They passed two ducks bathing in a puddle. To the right, the wild grasses ended, and a field of brown and bent corn stalks sprang up.

A fat cricket scuttled across the road. As they went by, he chirped them a farewell song. Nearing the top of the rise, as Marcel turned to give the friendly fellow a wave goodbye, he bumped into Scamp and nearly bowled her over.

"Watch it, Spike!" she barked.

"Sorry," he replied. "Why did we stop? Are you hungry too?" He was hoping this was the case. He was more than ready for a snack.

Scamp pointed at the ground in front of them. "That. That's why we stopped."

Marcel looked to where she was pointing. "I don't see anything."

"Exactly," said the little mouse. "The trail dried up. The stink-water's gone."

Marcel looked again and felt his stomach sink. The last drips of paint *had* been few and far between. They stood over the last golden drop and stared at it. "What now?" he asked.

"We use our noggins," Scamp announced. "We gotta listen to our common sense."

"What does it say?" asked Marcel.

"What does it . . . ?" Scamp fixed two piercing eyes on his. "You see any trucks growing wings and flying off lately? We keep to the road, of course!"

Marcel's cheeks pinked. "Oh. Right."

Scamp turned and began to hike the last few steps to the top of the hill. "Forget the nose—use your noggin! That's what I always say. A mind's got all sorts of ideas! Not that anybody listens to the smallest mouse. It really wasn't my fault. Accidents just happen sometimes, you know? Who knew soybeans were so flammable? But my brain says we just follow this road and—" She stopped walking.

At the top of the ridge, Scamp stared ahead, mouth slightly open, her words still dangling from the tip of her tiny pink tongue. Marcel climbed the last few steps and followed her gaze.

On the other side of the hill, the road fell away . . .

And dissolved into a knot of roads, three of them, sprinting off in every direction.

"Ohhh," breathed Marcel.

Scamp swallowed. "A minor setback. Shouldn't be a problem. We'll . . . we'll just, uh, sniff it out when we get to the fork. Yeah." She gave a little cough. "It's like I always say: the nose always knows!"

"But I thought you said—"

"The nose always knows *sometimes*, Marcel."

It took patience, but the trek downhill was far easier than the climb. By the time they reached the crossing, the sun was an angry fireball in the sky, low and sinking lower. The light was fading.

The mouse and the hedgehog and his cocoon stood in the middle of the cross section of country road. They surveyed each option carefully. Scamp sniffed so deeply her whiskers curled up her nose. "Well? What do you smell? Any stink-water?"

Marcel closed his eyes and took in a long whiff.

The scent of a million moldering corncobs.

Something rotten, but sweet—an apple core, perhaps.

A pine forest. Or a pine air freshener. One of the two. And . . .

Was it . . . ?

Popcorn?

Marcel sniffed again, and this time his eyes went wide behind the rims of his glasses. "Popcorn!" he cried. This was different from a cornfield or corncobs. It was: "Buttered popcorn! I'd know that smell anywhere!" And he would. Marcel knew that smell better than any nose in the world.

"Popcorn?" Scamp said dubiously. She sniffed again too. "You mean . . . *whizzlepop*?"

Now it was Marcel's turn to question. "Whizzle-pop?"

"Yeah, you know. When corn *whizzle*s over the fire, then *pop*s into a flower? *Whizzlepop!*"

Marcel giggled. "I call it popcorn. But I like whizzlepop, too."

"I smell it," said Scamp. "I do smell it."

Marcel stood on tiptoe and tried to catch another whiff. At length, a breeze came, and sure enough, the road to the right of them carried a distinct buttery air. "It's that way," said Marcel, pointing. "It smells like the theater. I think we go that way."

Scamp looked at him, one eyebrow cocked. "You sure?"

"I'm sure," answered Marcel. "I think I'm sure."

Scamp nodded. "Sounds sensical to me."

They turned down the popcorn-scented road, following their noses, trusting their instincts.

They hadn't traveled far before the light became too hard to see by.

"Do you think we should stop?" Marcel asked.

"'Course not," said Scamp, hiking up her belt.

But five steps and a stumble later Scamp piped up again. "Here's good. Let's stop for the night. We can sleep just inside the cornfield there. The road'll be there in the morning."

Scamp did seem to change her mind a lot, Marcel thought.

But relieved at the prospect of food and rest, Marcel put it out of mind. Soon they were scouring up dinner, filling their bellies, fluffing corn husks for beds, and settling in as the last light melted away.

Marcel tucked Toto under a husk close to his side. Scamp used her cape as a blanket and lay on her back, gazing past the cornstalks into the starry night. She shivered.

"Harvest is almost over," she murmured. "It'll

be harder to catch up once the snow's here."

Marcel thought about this. He'd never had to worry about finding and storing food for winter. The theater had an endless supply of Cinnamon Snaps and Coco-nutties, heaps of Fruit Gems (lime). How much did a whole village of mice need? And for an entire winter?

"Did the Mousekins stop up that leaking log, you think?" he asked.

Scamp didn't answer right away. "Probably. Not that it's enough. They don't tell me much, but we've only got enough to last about half the winter."

"But everyone was working so hard."

"We're behind. We've had to move five times this year," Scamp explained.

"Why?"

"Reasons," Scamp mumbled. "They weren't *all* my fault."

"That must've been a lot of work." Marcel knew what it was like to move a lot, but he'd never taken a whole town with him.

Scamp scoffed at this. "Everyone's so busy,

they probably don't even realize I'm gone."

Marcel frowned, confused. "But you told your father, remember?"

"Right," Scamp said softly. "Sure I told him. Anyway, quit being so nosy."

Something howled far away. They froze and listened.

All that sounded was the wind in the corn.

But now Marcel's mind was turning. Night in the city was one thing. Night in the country was quite another. Foxes, coyotes, *snakes* . . .

"I was wondering," he whispered to the mouse. "Do you think there are snakes around here too? And could you tell me more about the milk snake? The one my box dropped on? Oona said she was like a—a witch. Well, was she?"

"There's only one witch in these parts," Scamp answered matter-of-factly.

Wondering what she meant, Marcel peeked over at Scamp. She didn't say anything for a while.

"It would've worked, you know," she said finally. "My idea."

Marcel lay very still, listening.

"The fire was a bad idea—you can't control it. But my *pulley* . . . ," said Scamp.

"Pulley?"

"Yeah, I call it a pulley, because you pull things up . . . or lower them down. But I call it a pulley."

"Like an elevator," said Marcel.

"It's my invention," Scamp said. "Anyway, I sewed this net and attached it to the pulley, so that when the milk snake came sneaking around, I'd *trap* her."

"Wow."

"Mice have all sorts of things that hunt them. Snakes, and worse things. You can't always run away. Sometimes you gotta fight!"

"So why didn't you?" asked Marcel. "Why didn't you trap the snake?"

Scamp rubbed at her eyes. She scratched ferociously at a spot on her chin. She turned on her side away from him.

"You beat me to it" was the last thing Marcel heard her say.

✦ ✦ ✦

Something woke him.

He wasn't sure what. But something definitely woke him.

Marcel sat up in the dark and put on his glasses. Scamp lay next to him, curled under her leaf-cape, snoring. Marcel grabbed Toto and crept to a nearby spot where the cornstalks opened up a little further and looked up at the sky.

The stars winked at him coldly.

They always did.

He was about to turn away, when, in a flash, a group of stars seemed to blow out and flare again. Something whipped by. A leaf, perhaps? A bird? Marcel blinked and felt his quills prickle.

Was something there? He listened hard but heard nothing. Just the cackle of corn husks.

His heart began to beat fast. A sudden fear trickled down his spine.

"Scamp?" he called timidly.

Suddenly Marcel felt a sharp wind above, and

he rolled quickly into a ball. Something grazed his face.

His glasses. They were on his face, and now they weren't.

He heard them drop to the dirt somewhere behind him. Had something—the wind?—snatched them up just then. Or . . .

Someone.

A patter of quick feet sounded at his back. Marcel thought he might faint.

"Get up, you horse chestnut! *Run!*"

Marcel popped out of a ball just as Scamp tore past, tossing him his glasses. By a stroke of blind luck, he caught them.

"Get up!" Scamp screamed over her shoulder. Marcel obeyed.

But not before he knew why.

Scamp ran as though lightning were licking her tail.

"The witch!" she screamed. "It's *Wickedwing*!"

CHAPTER 8

Bucket of Rust

THEY RAN. PAST A MILLION CORNSTALKS. THIS way, that. Left and right.

They ran and ran and ran.

The ground tore at Marcel's feet. His lungs ached. He feared he hadn't strapped Toto tight enough beneath his chin. He wouldn't lose the little cocoon.

More than once Marcel felt a very real presence at his back. Something nearly upon him. But he raced on, Scamp ahead, her tail flying pin straight behind her.

"There! Up there!" Scamp shouted. "I see something!"

In the dark ahead, in a small clearing, a large object glinted silvery and green under the stars. They ran for it.

The great hulk of an old tractor lay wounded in the field, one monstrous wheel broken beneath it, the other bracing the body but leaving it grossly aslant. Tall weeds grew up and around and through it. "Get in!" yelled Scamp as she barreled through the weeds and up the tractor's iron belly.

They flew into the clanging guts of the beast. Scamp poked around easily, quickly finding a black cavity, which they tumbled inside. They froze. Hearts racing, two sets of ears pricked up lickety-split, listening for any sign of whatever was chasing them.

The only sound was their hammering chests. And then . . .

Clank . . . clang . . . donggggg . . . scratch. Something clanked heavily against the metal skin of the tractor—the sound of clawed feet. The tractor groaned. Marcel held his breath.

It felt like hours before he let it go.

The two travelers (and Toto) waited. Listened. Wrung their paws. At the sound of doves and sparrows twittering in the corn, there was a crunch of dried leaves. Scamp leaned back against the cold metal beside him. "I think she's gone," she said, sighing deeply. "The birds. They wouldn't be singing if she were close."

Toto wriggled against Marcel's chest, and Marcel laid a hand on the little pouch to make sure Toto was okay after the night's ordeal. "That was—that was—" Marcel could barely bring himself to say it. "The witch?"

Scamp was fiddling with something in the dark next to her. "Yes," she answered. "*That* was Wickedwing."

Marcel didn't like the sound of this at all. It was a little too much like *The Wizard of Oz*'s Wicked Witch. Marcel swallowed. "And what *is* she?"

"What do you mean what is she? She's Wickedwing."

"I know, but, well, she's real, isn't she?" asked Marcel.

"'Course she's real!" hollered Scamp. "Are you thick?"

"But . . . well, she's a real witch? I mean she had wings, I think. . . ."

"Well, how else is she gonna fly?"

"She's an *OWL*!" boomed a low, scratchy voice at the other side of the chamber.

Scamp screeched. Marcel popped into a ball.

There was a rustling of leaves as the voice continued. "She's an owl, you blockheads, and you brought her right to my house!"

"I'm not a blockhead," Marcel heard Scamp say.

"I move to the middle of a cornfield to get away from all this nonsense," the voice went on. A clang and a creak reverberated through the chamber as a small window opened and sent in a faint shaft of sunlight. "And nonsense finds me anyway."

Marcel's eyes took a second to adjust, but when they did, he watched as an old gray squirrel propped a small twig under the window hatch and turned to look at them. "Eh," said the squirrel. "You're kids. Makes it worse. Means half the town will be here looking for you before long."

Scamp was a mess. Her fur was caked with mud. Her grass belt was tattered, and her walnut-shell shield was askew. "You live here?" she asked the squirrel.

"No. I just wait for critters to show up so I can cook them breakfast," snapped the squirrel. "Yes, I live here. At least I did until you two showed up. Now old owl-eyes will be all over the place." He stomped over to a heaping pile of acorns, hickory nuts, and corn and filled his arms.

Scamp frowned. "So, you're leaving, then?"

The squirrel paused. "What? No, I'm not leaving. I'm making breakfast!"

Blockheads. Nonsense. Kids. The squirrel certainly seemed to think little of them. It was obvious they weren't welcome. And as Scamp mumbled to herself, her dark eyes following the squirrel's every move, Marcel wondered how often folks made Scamp feel as small as her size. She'd already made it clear her fellow Mousekins weren't prone to listen to *her*, the smallest mouse.

It was surprising, really. From Marcel's perspective, Scamp was larger than life.

They watched as the old squirrel pried open nutshells and tossed what was inside out the window and onto a small scrap of tin warm with sun. Soon, the smell of roasting nuts filled the inside of the tractor.

The gray squirrel grumbled to himself. "Would you look at me. Serving all my hard work to a pack of hooligans. Should've booted 'em out and let the cornfield teach 'em a lesson." He collected the nuts from the pan and threw servings into two acorn caps. "Here!" he barked, sliding the bowls in front of them. "Eat something."

"Thank you," said Marcel softly.

"You shouldn't have," said Scamp, a fiendish look in her eye.

"I know I shouldn't have, but I did! And don't expect a thing more. Got a rust bucket for a heart"—the squirrel thumped a wiry paw against his chest—"so don't you bother me with your sob stories. I'm just feeding you so's you leave. The sooner you get out, the better!"

"Hrmph," said Scamp, but she polished off her nut greedily, bits and pieces speckling her face.

"And another thing," said the squirrel, absent-mindedly refilling Scamp's bowl. "Don't you think I'm gonna be sending anything with you when you go. You got miles of corn out there, and I spent weeks bringing these nuts here from the forest—they're mine!" He realized then that he'd unknowingly given the mouse another helping. Just as Scamp brought the acorn to her mouth, the squirrel snatched it away and threw it in his cheek, his eyes bulging.

Scamp chomped hard on the ghost of that mouth-watering morsel, and when she realized what'd happened, she threw the old squirrel the iciest of glares.

The squirrel gave one authoritative nod. "Hrmph," he grunted, the nut still tucked in his cheek.

They stayed like that, the two eyeballing each other, until Marcel finished his breakfast.

The squirrel broke the silence. "The owl you two brought here—she's in for the night. You can be on your way now."

Scamp didn't hesitate. "Come on, Marcel. Let's get out of this tin can." She turned on her tail and scrabbled out, swiping a few nuts as she went.

When Marcel met her outside the tractor, Scamp's eyes were ablaze. "That old bristle-tail! Good riddance!" she said as she stuffed the stolen nuts in her sack.

Marcel gasped. "But the squirrel said he didn't want to give us any—"

"Oh, *scat* what the squirrel said," Scamp snapped. "See if I care! He's awful. He's got no heart! In place of a heart, he's got a rock. A walnut shell! His heart's just like this junk heap—an *empty ol' tin can*!"

Something struck Marcel. Hard. Scamp's words. *Heart. Tin can.* What was it about them that sounded so familiar?

Heart . . . Tin . . .

The Tin Man! From *The Wizard of Oz*! The Tin

Man had gone to the Wizard in search of a heart!

How incredible this all was! Here Marcel was on a journey to get to the Emerald City (a theater, but still), first landing in Mousekinland of all places, killing the snake and meeting Oona—Oona who reminded him so much of Glinda—running from a witch named Wickedwing, and now a squirrel like the Tin Man, a squirrel lacking a heart. If only Scamp were like the Scarecrow. Then he'd really be amazed.

Wait.

Scamp *was* like the Scarecrow. She literally *scared crows* off with her slingshot.

Scamp flung her sack over her shoulder and eyed Marcel. "Well? You coming, prickle-puss?"

Marcel bit his lip.

"Don't you worry. I know what I'm doing. I might be the smallest, but I know things," Scamp said. She tapped her nose. "The nose knows, you know. We gotta be close now! Just need another whiff of that whizzlepop." She dove into a patch of grass. A few seconds later, Marcel's sack full of

Fruit Gems burst out of the weeds and landed at his feet. Scamp must've snagged the sack during the chase last night. A few Gems toppled out.

Marcel hurriedly scooped up the loose Gems and stuffed them back inside, praying Scamp's nose hadn't sniffed them out. He quickly straightened and tried to look innocent.

Scamp popped back out of the grass. "Whizzle-pop, here we come! Come on, Marcel! Grab your rocks!"

Marcel grabbed his sack. He paused.

In the movie, Dorothy and the Scarecrow *had* made it to the Emerald City in the end. But . . .

Marcel gulped.

It was the flying monkeys, witches, and wizards he was a little concerned about all of a sudden.

But the hens, Marcel told himself. *Auntie Hen, Uncle Henrietta . . .*

They were worth it.

Marcel adjusted his spectacles bravely. And for the first time, he noticed that the left pane of his glasses—the one that was cracked when he fell into Mousekinland—was no longer there. (This did not feel reassuring.)

In fact, it felt downright ominous.

"Where are you headed?" a voice demanded. The old squirrel scrambled out of the bones of the green and silver tractor and into the weedy clearing.

Scamp whirled around and hugged her stolen sack of acorns. "Why?"

"Because I've been listening to you two nincompoops and realize I'm going to have to *get* you to wherever it is you're going if I want peace and quiet around here. If you go off on your own, you'll only walk in circles and come barging your way back." The squirrel crossed his arms stiffly. "Well? Where to?"

Standing there, statue-like, and shining silver in the sun, the squirrel looked so much like the Tin Man, Marcel at once felt certain he was meant to join them. He stumbled forward. Introductions first.

"Hello," he said, putting out a paw. "We haven't

been properly introduced. I'm Marcel. I'd like to thank you for sharing your breakfast."

Introductions first. *Manners* second.

The squirrel eyed Marcel's outstretched paw. A frown crimped his brow. "Hrmph," he said after a minute. "Ingot. The name's Ingot." He gave Marcel's paw a firm shake.

Marcel dragged Scamp over. "And this is Scarlet—that's what her father named her—but *we* call her Scamp. We're trying to get to the Emerald City Theater." He placed Scamp's paw in Ingot's, and the two shook. Reluctantly.

(It was a pitiful sight.)

"And this is Toto." Marcel motioned to the cocoon.

"A cocoon?" exclaimed an angry-sounding Ingot. "Well, this day couldn't get any weirder, now, could it? So. We got a hedgehog—with goggles, I might add—a cocoon strapped to his belly, a right scrap of a mouse, and something called the Emerald City—that's it?" He looked to the sky. "I've seen it all now."

Yes, that was it in a nutshell.

Marcel found himself smiling.

Him toting Toto. Scrappy Scamp blazing trails and scaring crows. On their way to the Emerald City. It was all so familiar.

"That's exactly right," said Marcel.

"It's weird," said Ingot.

Scamp glowered at the squirrel. "He didn't ask you what you thought of it."

"No, he certainly didn't, but I'm old and I tell people what I think." Ingot shot up an eyebrow. "And you're young and one of the smallest things I ever did see—but what a mouth."

Marcel wasn't fond of arguing, and anyway, he was buoyed by the thought that maybe, just maybe, they were on the right track. He didn't want to lose a moment's time. He took control of the situation before things got out of hand. "What do you think, Ingot? Can you get us back to the road?" he asked.

"The road? Certainly can't," the squirrel answered. "The way to the road is snake territory.

Don't know quite how you made it all the way out to me, but you go that way, you meet your grave, sure enough."

Marcel's buoyed thoughts capsized and sank. And a wisp of worry, like a tiny bug, landed on his heart.

Scamp balked. "But we have to go that way! That's the where the whizzlepop smell was coming from! Marcel *has* to get there, that's the way, and I'm taking him!"

"You're welcome to try it. Won't bother me either way. I told you," said Ingot. He thumped his chest. "Nothing but a rust bucket right here. Ticker quit working right a long time ago! Go ahead, risk it if you like. But I won't be helping you."

Scamp looked off in the direction of the road.

"Long way. Lots of snakes," said Ingot. He nodded to the north. "I'll take you as far as the forest. Road cuts through there. On the other side's where you'll find your city. I've seen it myself. You'll make it in three days."

"I don't think I believe you," Scamp told him.

Marcel and Ingot watched as the mouse ran to a tall, sturdy cornstalk, scaled it to the top, and propped herself against a wrinkled ear of corn and a drab leaf. Lacy clouds slipped by as Scamp scanned the horizon, high above the field.

At length, Scamp's shoulders slumped. She climbed down and jumped from the last leaf to the ground. "I can't find the road," she said to Marcel bitterly. "He's right about the woods. They're off to the north—well, north*west*."

She turned to face Ingot, stomped to the spot beneath his nose, and looked up into his gray face. "You better be right about the city, squirrel."

"I'm right," said Ingot.

"Better be! Just look at him." Scamp gestured to Marcel dramatically. "He's unarmed! He needs me to help him get back to his hens! We made a deal."

"Deal?" asked Ingot. "What deal was that?"

"None of your beeswax," answered Scamp. "Your only concern should be helping me get this horse chestnut where he needs to go. I *have* to."

Something about the way she said it made Marcel feel better. Lighter. Expectant.

Scamp cared.

And for a second, that little worry-bug on his heart grew wings and took flight.

CHAPTER 9

Nothing Breeds Melancholy Like a Marsh

AFTER MARCEL REFUSED TO GO ANYWHERE until the others promised to try to get along, he and his companions trudged through the cornfield for the remains of the day, hiding once from a patrolling hawk and another time stopping to let Scamp dry after she traipsed into a deep puddle and disappeared.

Scamp chattered away, telling Marcel all about Mousekinland's many moves. As a result, she was very familiar with all sorts of terrain and harsh environments.

"Settled near train tracks once—until our eyes

turned yellow. Mice don't take well to soot in their food. Then there was the stone bridge over the river. Too wet. Especially after I pulled out a pebble for my sling-shooter and the whole thing came falling down. But I don't really see how that was my fault. *Clearly*, the bridge had problems. It was bound to come down anyway." Scamp went on. "The quarry—just rocks, no food. I had my pulley system I wanted to try to set up to deliver supplies, but no one listens to the smallest mouse. And then there was the farmhouse—"

"We'll make camp in the marsh near the edge of the forest," interrupted Ingot. He'd led the way with nary a comment till now, a walking stick steadying his feet.

Scamp looked wary. "The marsh?"

"Sounds nice," said Marcel.

"There's an old gopher hole we can stay in for the night."

"*Gopher hole*?" questioned Scamp. "You ever seen the teeth on those things? That doesn't seem—"

Ingot whirled around and tapped the side of his head. "Got a brain? Use it. It's the gopher hole or owl bait. You pick."

Scamp's eyes fluttered wide. She backed away.

"Sorry," mumbled an embarrassed-looking Ingot. "That wasn't called for. I haven't been around folks for—for a while. I've gotten bad at this. Sorry."

Scamp's eyes narrowed. She pursed her lips and scratched at her cheek. She said nothing.

It was dark by the time they reached the marsh, and their nerves were raw as they crept through the shadows. Corn sprang up like a battlement all around, the crown of the forest barely visible on one side. But here the marsh spanned wide and meandering. Tall clumps of reeds waved next to black waters reflecting a universe of stars. There was even a tree or two on a few small hillocks, spindly and stunted, holding on to their last autumn leaves. From murky islands, pickerel frogs belched. The chirps of peepers throbbed into the cooling air. A few yards away, a dozen geese, noses tucked under their wings, roosted on reedy beds by the water.

"Over here," Ingot directed. "Been empty for as long as I've known of it." He led them to a swollen patch of ground where a scraggy maple perched. Grass grew up at its base, and it took a few minutes for Ingot to clear away the entrance to the hole. "Take some grass in with you," he told them. "It's bound to be damp in there."

More dank than damp it was, with just enough room for all of them to sleep comfortably apart, Marcel thought as he settled inside.

Scamp chose the far corner and went back and forth a few times with loads of grass. When she was sufficiently pleased with the size of her bed, she glanced over at Ingot and opened her mouth but quickly shut it and looked away.

Ingot, who'd been clearing a little rubble near the entrance of the hole, turned to them. His eyes shifted to one side and then the other. "I don't imagine you're hungry with all the corn we managed to scrape up today. But if you're thirsty, there's a small spring over by the tallest clump of reeds to the right. Just listen for the peepers. If they're singing, the coast is clear. If they stop—hide."

He scrambled out of the hole but popped his head back in before he turned and ran off. "You'll be fine on your own for a bit. Just listen for the peepers."

Scamp let out a long breath when he was gone. "I thought he'd never leave! Least he told us where we could find fresh water. Had us walking all day, and all I got was a swallow of mud! I don't like him, Marcel. He's—he's—"

"Old?" offered Marcel.

Scamp gave him a queer look. "No. Mean!" She dug into her sack and pulled out a tiny rose hip, hollowed into a cup. "I'm positively parched! Let's go find that spring!"

The water bubbled up colder and sweeter than any he'd ever tasted, and Marcel took drink after drink when they found it. He hadn't realized how thirsty he'd gotten. It was like that first taste of syrupy green soda from the cup he'd found behind the theater that last long day on the streets. He'd drunk it down in one gulp . . .

And got a merciless stomachache.

The last thing he'd needed was a sour stomach and a hot sidewalk. You had to be nimble on the streets to avoid the footsteps, the blaring cars, the stray cats. What he wanted was cool air. A place to rest. Something plush and comfortable, like one of Dorothy's pillow forts.

It was an air-conditioned breeze that caught his attention. And a whiff of popcorn.

The broken air shaft.

He'd followed it, and once he'd found his way inside, it was the velvet seat of 6HH that gave him comfort.

The lemon drops, lollipops, and Licorice Twists filled his belly.

The marathon of movies soothed his nerves.

He never went back to the streets.

Marcel took another drink and tried to forget.

Never would he have imagined he'd be this far from . . . *everything*.

Scamp was now perched over the spring, lapping up water, her rose-hip cup tossed aside. When she finished, her stomach gave a furious rumble. She groaned. "I think I drank too fast. My stomach hurts."

"You should probably lie down," Marcel told her.

The peepers were in full chorus as they tramped through the grasses, and by the time they got back to the hole, Scamp was complaining less and yawning more. (She'd also belched, which seemed to help.) They climbed inside and settled onto their grassy beds. Marcel looked over at Ingot's. It was empty.

"Don't you fret, Marcel," Scamp was saying between yawns. "He'll go back to his old rust heap and we'll get ourselves through the forest. By tomorrow night you'll be inches away from your city. I got a good feeling."

Marcel had every confidence in Scamp. But something began to worry him.

The plan—it was to find the popcorn scent. If they followed it, it would surely lead him back to the theater, wouldn't it? But what if . . . ? What if . . . ?

He felt the question explode in his mind like a popcorn kernel.

What if it doesn't and I'm back on the lonely streets of the city in search of another place I'll never find? He couldn't bear that.

Not again.

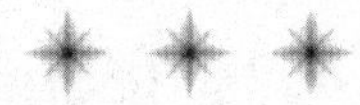

A piece of grass tickled his nose, and Marcel woke with a sneeze. He rubbed his eyes.

In her corner, Scamp was snoring (loudly), and across the way, moonlight lit up Ingot's empty bed.

What time was it? How long had the squirrel been gone?

Marcel crept over and felt Ingot's grassy mattress. It was cold.

At the entrance of the hole, Marcel tried calling. "Ingot?"

There was no answer.

Outside, the peepers sang heartily, but still

Marcel studied the sky before he stole out of the hole toward a safe snaggle of swamp grass a little way off.

What if the old gray squirrel had gotten lost somehow? What if he was caught in a tangle of marsh weed? What if he was hurt?

What if he left?

"Ingot?" Marcel called again, quieter this time. "Ingot, where are you?" He shivered, remembering the chase the night before. But surely . . .

But surely, if Wickedwing *had* been on the hunt . . .

He'd already be dinner.

Marcel ventured as far from the hole as he dared with no sign of the squirrel. He'd nearly given up and was on his way back to the hole when a glimmer of light on the marsh water caught his attention.

The night was windless, with only a few raggedy clouds, and the moon seemed to watch him as Marcel carefully crept through the reeds at the water's edge to get a better look.

Marcel poked his nose between a patch of grass . . .

And immediately pulled it back, stifling a startled screech.

Just a few yards away, across the water on the edge of a mossy rock, stood Ingot. His head was bowed. Not a hair on his grizzled coat moved. He held a single white flower cupped in his paws.

Marcel felt something twist in his chest. The way Ingot looked just now—it felt familiar to him. There was a sadness there that Marcel recognized. He stole another look.

Ingot spoke. "I don't want to—" He paused.

Who was Ingot speaking to? Marcel wondered.

"Stayed away all these years," Marcel heard him say. "And none of this is in my job description anymore. It cost too much."

Marcel held his breath.

Ingot bent down and rested the flower on the glassy pond. Slowly, slowly, ever so slowly, it floated out across the water and disappeared. Ingot stood watching for a moment. He groaned.

"I know what you'd say, though. *But if* you *don't help them, who will?*"

Ingot shook his head. "You were always right," he said quietly. "Give the kids a kiss for me. I've got some packing to do. Just in case." He turned and disappeared through the grass.

Marcel waited, listening to the squirrel swish through the dry reeds. Ingot didn't appear to be headed back toward the hole they'd borrowed. Marcel wondered where he was off to.

And who he'd been talking to.

It didn't appear to be . . . *anyone*.

As Marcel waited for the swishing to die away, his eyes drifted back to the spot where the squirrel had stood. Maybe a better look was what he needed. Was someone really there? And where had the flower gone?

He crept to the moss-covered rock, and what he saw there made him gasp.

Hundreds of the brittle white blooms from a nearby field of wildflowers floated with the stars reflected on the marsh waters.

The flowers. The *stars*. His heart pinched again.

Behind him, a voice spoke. "It's awfully late to be up."

Marcel spun around.

Behind him sat Oona, her green wings shining.

"Oona! You're back! I knew you'd come back!" he cried.

She fluttered over to him, and her dark eyes sparkled. "I've been looking for you, Marcel! I'm sorry I took so long."

"I don't mind," said Marcel. "You're here now."

"I didn't think you would," Oona said, smiling. "How are you, Marcel? How's your journey to the city?"

Marcel thought a moment. "Well, it's been . . . eventful."

"Eventful in a good way, I hope," Oona replied, and Marcel's heart swelled.

How glad he was that Oona was here! Green and glowing like she was, Marcel thought her more beautiful than Oz and all its brilliance. And how she reminded him of kind Glinda!

"Oona?" he tried. "Have you come to help me now—help me get back to the theater?"

The moth gave him a sad sort of smile. Her voice was quiet. "No, Marcel. Not in the way you'd like, I'm afraid. What you're asking isn't that easy."

"Oh." At her words, something inside Marcel deflated.

He'd been thinking about something for a little while now. Since he'd lived in the theater, he'd seen an awful lot of movies, and a movie journey was usually pretty easy at first. But somewhere around the middle and all the way to the end, things always got hard if you were one of the characters.

"The rest of the way," he asked Oona. "Do you think it will be dangerous?"

"I don't know, Marcel." Oona's eyes were soft. She thought for a moment. "But maybe we're not meant to. To know, that is. If we knew every turn of the journey before we set out . . ." She smiled. "Well, I wonder if we'd ever want to take that first step. Or that first flight, if you were me."

Her wings opened. Closed. This close to her,

Marcel noticed something. There was a tear in one wing. Long and ragged. It split the wing almost in two. He wondered why he hadn't noticed it before.

"In my experience, journeys haven't been easy, Marcel," Oona went on. "But if there's one thing I've learned, it's that a friend is never far away."

Marcel looked at her, her scarred wings drinking in all the light of the moon. The green of them like lime Fruit Gems and springtime and Oz and, now that he thought of it, Dorothy's stars. Dorothy's million glow-in-the-dark stars.

A mouse-size snore echoed out of the nearby gopher hole and rippled over the waters.

"I see *you've* found some friends," said Oona.

Marcel nodded, grateful. He had found friends. He wasn't alone. Not right now.

"I came to make sure you're all right," said Oona. "Are you all right?"

"I think so." Marcel was quiet for some time as together they stared out over the dark water. "I wanted to see where the flower went," he said after a little while.

"Oh?"

Marcel thought about it. Why *did* he? What was so important about Ingot's flower? And why did something tell him that there was so much more to Ingot's story than he knew. "I guess I wanted to stand here and see what my friend Ingot saw."

"Have you?"

Marcel realized something. "No. I don't think so. But . . ." Marcel hesitated. "The way Ingot looked—I didn't see what he saw, but I think maybe I know what he saw."

"What's that?" asked the moth. "What did he see?"

Marcel swallowed. "Something—something he lost."

Oona looked at him intently. "I think you're very wise for a hedgehog," she said. "And have you lost something like that too?""

Marcel was taken aback. "I—I've lost Auntie Hen and Uncle Henrietta. I lost the theater. And now the popcorn smell and the road. I've lost . . ."

I've lost Dorothy.

Oona's voice was warm. Movie-theater-butter warm. "Will you find it?"

He wasn't exactly sure which lost thing she might be asking about, so he answered the only way he knew how. "I'm trying to get back to the theater now."

The moth's eyes were kind. "That's not what I asked."

"I'm trying to find it—the theater. And the hens, you know, they live there with me. . . ."

Oona was quiet. She placed a furry foot on Marcel's. "I think you *have* lost something, Marcel, my hedgehog friend."

He had. He'd lost Dorothy. Lost her forever.

"But I wonder if one of the things you've lost isn't the most important thing you need to find—something you need more than all the rest. Not someone, not somewhere. It's not what you think."

"It's not? But what else is there?" he asked, as Oona stretched out her wings.

"I think you'll find it," she said simply. "Sometimes you can't know what you've lost until it's sitting right there in front of you."

Oona pumped her wings, caught the wind, and began to fly away.

"Will I see you again?" Marcel called after her.

Oona's answer floated back out over the water. "I *hope* so, Marcel! I'll certainly try! But I do hope we find each other again!"

CHAPTER 10

Lions, Tigers, and Other Fearsome Beasts

MARCEL WAS STILL ASLEEP, BUT HE HAD THE feeling something was watching him. He cracked an eye open.

Two beady eyes hovered an inch from his own. He screamed.

Scamp stood over him, glaring, a fist on each hip. "You just gonna lie there like a thistle all day?" she complained. "It's past sunup! I've done sixteen and a half things already."

Marcel yawned.

He'd never completely gotten used to being awake during the day. He'd willed himself to be up for Dorothy, and theater life had required it. But how Scamp was always so . . . *awake* was a mystery.

He rolled to his feet and rubbed his tired eyes.

He'd returned without trouble after Oona's visit, but he'd lain awake long after—long enough to hear the old gray squirrel return in the wee hours of the morning. "I'm up," he said.

"Little bit of a thing," growled a squinting Ingot from a corner of the burrow. "Thinks she claps her paws and the sun stands at attention, that one. Reminds me of my . . ." He trailed off and got up slowly, gingerly, his back curving a few degrees more than it had the night before. "It's gonna take a little while to get these bones oiled and ready to go. Don't move like I used to."

Scamp was cramming corn into her pack and muttering to herself. She'd been out collecting supplies for the journey. She shot a sour look at Ingot.

"You look like you could use some help," said Marcel, bending over to collect a kernel from the hollow's dirt floor.

Scamp snatched it away, a pained look crossed

her face. "Why does everyone think I can't handle things? I know what I'm doing!"

"Oh, I know that," Marcel tried to reassure her. "I just didn't want you to have to do all the work."

"I know what I'm doing," Scamp snapped back, scratching at her cheek again.

She seemed to scratch whenever she got upset, Marcel realized.

"Well," said Ingot, eyebrows raised. "Now that we've got *that* squared away." He grabbed his walking stick and a small corn-husk satchel Marcel hadn't seen the day before and arranged it across his chest. "We got about an hour's journey to the forest. I'll get you to the first line of trees. Then, uh—" He cleared his throat. "Then you're on your own."

"On our own is how me and Marcel like it," answered Scamp.

The early-morning temperature made clouds of their breath, but the sun worked at the cold, so that by the time the travelers—Ingot, Scamp, Marcel (and Toto)—came upon the line of trees that marked the western woods, they were almost toasty.

Red spruce, hickory, and pine stood like sentinels and steady as the passage of time. Marcel stretched up on tiptoe trying to see farther than the first hundred or so steps into the wood, but it was difficult. The whole of the forest was craggy and unkempt. Hill became valley; mound dropped to pit. Nowhere was there an inch of smooth ground. Nowhere at all.

Ingot, who'd been in the lead, turned to face them. "Here we are. I recommend climbing that spruce there. If you travel north and to the west, you shouldn't run out of good branches to jump to."

Scamp's jaw dropped. "You've got to be kidding."

Marcel looked down at his short legs. "I've never climbed a tree," he whispered.

Toto, Marcel thought, gave a shudder.

But Ingot was still talking. "Sure as sugar maple. North—northwest you want to go. Midway you should find a good stand of old fruit trees. Might think about stopping for a bite to eat at that point.

You'll at least find a few friendly faces. Tell 'em Gov—tell 'em *Ingot* sent you."

"Your brain has turned to sawdust," said Scamp.

"What Scamp means," said Marcel, "is that though, technically, she might be able to climb that tree there, it seems unlikely either of us would be able to jump from tree to tree." He tried jumping a little for effect and, without meaning to, tumbled over on his side.

"Sawdust," repeated Scamp.

"Well," said a satisfied-looking Ingot. "Looks like you two'll just have to head on home then. You've had your adventure. Time to be done with this nonsense."

Scamp gasped. "This was your plan all along? You've been lying to us this whole time? Are we even close to the city?" she squeaked.

"You're clos*er*," said Ingot. "But there's no way you could ever make it through on foot. It's time to head home, kids."

Scamp pushed past him, scrambling atop a fallen pine just beyond the tree line. She hiked up her belt and patted her sling-shooter. "Don't worry, Marcel. I can handle this. *I'll* take you through the forest." She turned on her heel and began to go deeper into the brush and trees.

Marcel gave Ingot a small smile and shrugged. He secured his spectacles and Toto and took a few steps after the mouse when, in a blink, the old gray squirrel ran up behind Scamp and overtook her.

Ingot stood in a narrow passage between two fallen tree limbs, blocking Scamp's path. Ingot looked down at her sternly, the scruff of his neck standing on end. "You're stubborn, I'll give you that. Thought you two would've turned back by now. But"—he growled—"you two have no idea the surprises these trees can hold, the things they hide. You can't just go for a stroll in there. Jumping tree to tree is one thing. Taking the forest by foot is quite another!"

"I don't see how it's any of your business," said Scamp. "You made it perfectly clear you're not going to help us, and we've got no problem going it alone! The forest can't be that fearsome."

Ingot glowered at her. "What do you know of it? You've no idea what's beyond these trees! Never seen a thing." His voice got very quiet. "Well, I have. I've seen things. And there's more than just a few snakes in the woods."

"I know danger!" Scamp spat back. She threw down her sling-shooter with a fierce *thwap*. "You—you and everyone else think I don't know anything! But I'm not stupid and little! You don't know the things I've seen—the things I've done! Snakes, crows, *Wickedwing*! I once set a whole field on fire trying to scare off a family of weasels! While everyone else is so worried about storing enough food to eat, *I'm* the one making sure *they* don't get eaten!" Scamp sniffed. "They won't even let me have a sword!"

Marcel watched the look of surprise on Ingot's face turn to a weary resignation.

Scamp began to scratch. "It's *you* that don't know!" she said, digging at a spot on her neck.

Ingot's brow creased. Something Scamp said seemed to sit heavily with him—too heavily.

"Maybe I was wrong. I shouldn't have judged," he said.

Scamp picked up her sling-shooter and tucked it slowly into her belt. "You shouldn't have," she said quietly.

Marcel looked down at his feet and swallowed hard.

Maybe this was all a mistake.

Neither the mouse nor Ingot would be here if it weren't for him. Was it wrong to ask Scamp to go on? With danger about and the woods to face? What about the old squirrel? Marcel could tell he was itching to get back to his tractor. Marcel was asking too much.

He thought about the movies again. At a certain point, in almost every movie, the main character always has to face his fears alone.

That must be now, Marcel thought.

Marcel spoke, and as he did, there was a tremble in his voice. "I'd like to thank you both for all you've done for me," he said. "You have been a good friend to me, Scamp. And, Ingot, thank you for helping. But I should probably go on by myself now—"

"You'll do no such thing," barked the old squirrel, just as Scamp said, "No way, bristle-butt!"

Ingot sighed and rolled his eyes. "If you insist on going, I'm coming with you. Couldn't hold my head up otherwise." He patted his satchel. "Already packed. What've I got to do anyway? I know this forest, these folk. I'll take you through." Without giving anyone room to argue, Ingot turned and began to make a path through the trees.

"If he's going, I'm going!" shouted Scamp, straightening her walnut-shell shield. "You can't get rid of me that easy! Besides, you need me, Marcel!" She ran after Ingot, cape fluttering out behind her.

Marcel looked down at Toto. "I guess we'll be going together. All of us."

And he had to admit, the relief he felt at that moment?

It was like flicking on a spotlight in the dark pitch of a theater.

They trekked long into the afternoon, stopping to drink from forest pools and once to rest their eyes at the top of a smooth, sunlit rock. Ingot stayed mostly silent throughout the day, hackles up and listening intently for every *crack* and *snap* of the woods. Scamp, however, seemed bent on chatting, spouting a litany of facts about fungi, fern, flora, fauna—every last leaf and pebble that caught her gaze. Marcel listened happily, grateful for the distraction.

The day was largely uneventful. Once, they happened upon a trio of fox kits playing near the entrance of their den but crept away without being seen.

When it came time for dinner, Ingot stopped under a giant of an oak and pointed to a few acorns scattered on the ground. "We can stop here for the night. You two'll have to fetch dinner. I . . ." He threw off his satchel and collapsed in the roots of the great tree. "I think my knees are done for today."

"Acorns are a good source of protein and vitamins for field mice," remarked Scamp. "The fat content in acorns is remarkably—"

"Hey, you with the mouth," said Ingot, pointing to the acorns lying about. "Quit your yammering and get on with it." He reached into his corn-husk satchel, pulled out a hollowed-out seed filled with some kind of salve, and rubbed the salve on his knees and ankles. "Dark will be here soon. We'll need to tuck in and be hidden before nightfall."

Marcel and Scamp settled their things in two comfortable crooks in the oak's roots. They'd do for beds later. Leaving the old squirrel behind, they went off to collect supper, one acorn at a time.

Scamp found two under a leafy fern. Marcel found one tucked into the tight roll of an oak leaf. They began to spread out from the base of the trunk. Scamp tried the soft brown drifts of pine needles near an old log, while Marcel followed an ant toward what he noted was a particularly dark and imposing pine tree a good acorn's throw away.

Then he saw something strange farther in. Something that didn't belong.

An enormous dead tree stood a little way off in a small clearing. Old grapevine and hairy ropes of poison ivy snaked over it, this way and that. A thick emerald moss enveloped the trunk underneath. A tangled mess, it was dark, infinitely creepy, and so very green.

Marcel crept into a sea of ferns, closer.

The air grew colder, the shadows longer.

As if drawn to the strange tree, Marcel took another step.

The forest went still.

"RAAAAAAAAAAAWR!"

Marcel was still a few yards away when he heard the dreadful growl. He immediately rolled into a ball, shivering with fright.

Snarling, a screech, and a hiss followed. The noise was terrifying in its pitch, its volume, its insistence.

"Hissssss . . . raaaaaaaaawr! . . . grrrrrrrrrrrr . . . ack, ack, ack!"

Ack?

Marcel heard Scamp run over to him as the growling continued, felt her pull at a leg sticking out from his prickly ball of hedgehog spines.

"Come on, Marcel! Run!" she shouted over each harrowing hiss. "You can't stay rolled in a ball! That fearsome creature's about to eat us! You gotta—" She paused. "Wait a minute. . . ."

Wait a minute?!!

Marcel stopped shaking and opened an eye in time to see Scamp creeping off toward the thick base of the strange tree and disappearing around the other side, sling-shooter at the ready.

"Come back!" he managed to squeak out.

"I see you!" Scamp shouted. "I see you, you . . . *beast*!"

"Scamp!" Marcel squeaked again.

He heard the sling-shooter fly. A pebble hit its mark. Then:

A tiny cry.

"Scamp!" Marcel called, and this time he forced himself toward the tree in search of his friend.

There was a hard *thump* and another cry as he rounded the other side.

"Gotcha, you—you"—Scamp was standing next to a very furry creature, three times her size—"you . . . raccoon?"

Marcel came closer.

It was. It was a baby raccoon. His wispy hair sprouted out in every direction, and humanlike hands covered his small, masked eyes.

The poor thing was shaking like a leaf and crying with all its might.

CHAPTER 11

A Tyke Named Tuffy (Who Was Not Very Tough-y)

SCAMP BENT CLOSE TO THE CURLED-UP AND CRYing raccoon, trying to comfort him.

"I didn't mean to hurt you. I just—well, you were growling and carrying on. I thought you were something that wanted to eat us. It shouldn't have hurt that bad. But then I guess you fell out of that weird tree, so maybe it did. But why were you sounding so awful?"

Marcel crept close too, and not quite sure what to do, he slowly and very carefully laid a paw on the raccoon's arm.

The raccoon seemed to relax a little, though he

continued to cry. It was a heart-wrenching sound. Marcel waited and tried to pump comforting feelings into the furry little arm.

After a while, the tyke's sobs turned to whimpers and then to weepy sighs.

Marcel took a deep breath. "It's okay. We won't hurt you. We're not very scary."

"Speak for yourself," said Scamp.

The raccoon stopped whimpering at once. He looked up and blinked at them.

"Hi," said Marcel.

Just then Ingot came bounding over the ferns, sending the raccoon into another fit of tears and trembling.

"I heard the commotion," Ingot shouted, out of breath and wheezing a bit. "What happened? Was it the owl?"

Marcel patted the raccoon. "Ingot, we found someone. A new friend."

"Uh. Yes. Hi—hello," said Ingot, looking a bit awkward. He seemed unable to keep his eyes on the crying raccoon. He shifted from foot to foot.

He looked to Marcel and Scamp. "He going to carry on like this all day?"

"You'd think we were bobcats. Or *bears* or something," said Scamp. "At least something with teeth bigger than apple seeds."

Bears. *Lions and tigers and bears, oh my.*

Marcel remembered the line. It came whirling back.

The woods. The growling. The wailing Cowardly Lion in *The Wizard of Oz*.

"He's a brave raccoon, I think," said Marcel, remembering the end of the movie and how the Lion, who had no more or less courage than the rest, felt a bit better when the Wizard gave him a medal.

Marcel plucked a thin, rubbery piece of fungus from the tree and plastered it onto the raccoon's fur.

"For meritorious conduct," Marcel recited, "extraordinary valor, and, uh, lionlike bravery against . . . against Scamp here, I award you this mushroom medal. You are now a member of the Mushroom Legion of Courage."

Yes, that was it. He'd remembered the words exactly. Nearly exactly.

Scamp gave Marcel a look like he'd lost his head. "What's a *lion*?"

It took Ingot a second to catch on. "Ah. Yes. Very brave. Indeed!" he agreed. "Congratulations!" Ingot was a budding thespian, Marcel could see.

The raccoon hesitantly took his hands away from his eyes and looked down at his medal.

"You two are off your—"

"Scamp!" yelled Ingot, interrupting the mouse. "Don't you think this *baby* raccoon is quite the tough guy for his age?" He turned his head away from the tyke and winked at her.

"You got dirt in your eye or something?" asked a dumbfounded Scamp. "Why do you keep winking at me?"

Ingot rolled his eyes, sighed heavily, and looked to Marcel.

Marcel sat next to the creature and used his softest voice. "Where's your family? Is your home nearby?" Marcel felt certain they'd hear the patter of raccoon feet momentarily. Surely the little raccoon's parents were out looking for him. He was far too small to be out in the woods alone.

The raccoon just blinked at him.

Marcel looked around. He perked up his ears. Nothing stirred except two sparrows flittering on a branch and a little wind in the pine boughs. Even Scamp was uncharacteristically quiet.

Somewhere in the distance, a crow cried.

Marcel turned back to the raccoon. "Your mother must be near. Would you like us to call her for you? You . . ." He hesitated. "You aren't *lost,* are you?" Marcel felt a chill go down his spine.

The raccoon stared at him again, and immediately his eyes filled with tears. He nodded.

A lump rose in Marcel's throat. "You're lost?"

The raccoon nodded again.

"For how long?" Marcel cried.

The little raccoon held up four furry fingers.

"Four minutes?" asked Marcel. The raccoon shook his head. "Four hours?"

The raccoon shook his head again.

"Four *days*?"

The raccoon nodded vigorously.

Marcel swallowed, and the lump caught in his throat. "Are you sure? You sure you didn't just get turned around a bit?"

"He said he was lost, you pine cone!" Scamp snapped. She scooted Marcel out of the way, faced the raccoon, and patted his fluffy shoulder. "Don't worry, guy. We'll take care of you."

She turned back and faced Ingot and Marcel and said quietly, "It's getting dark, and we can't go looking around in these conditions. What're we gonna do?"

"Darned if I know," Ingot whispered. "I certainly didn't sign up for this. I'm too old for excitement and I'm no good with babies. Marcel, got any bright ideas?"

Scamp nodded. "You *are* the only other lost one here."

"I . . . uh . . ." Marcel's thoughts swirled.

Lost.

The thing about the word "lost" was that it

meant different things depending on the way you used it.

Marcel *lost* a perfectly edible yogurt raisin once. He found it three months later.

Auntie Hen often had a *lost* look in her eyes. She was usually thinking about the last strawberry Fruit Gem she'd managed to scrounge up and was remembering its distinct not-quite-berry flavor.

Battles on the movie screen were won and *lost*.

So were soccer games. His Dorothy hadn't lost games often, but when she did, she stayed sad for a full ten minutes. (Marcel took at least twice as long.) He could hear her laughing at him, trying to cheer him up.

Come on, Marcel, don't be sad, she'd say. *There will be other games. You can't keep every ball out of the net.*

You win some, you lose some, Dorothy would tell him. *Just don't give up. Don't you ever give up. Persistence, Marcel! Mind over matter! If you give up after you lose, I guess it's sure you'll never win!*

She was amazing like that. It's why she won so

many more games than she lost. She was so very good at never, ever giving up.

But *lost* lost?

Marcel wasn't exactly sure where he was ever since he'd landed in Mousekinland, but he was headed back. Headed somewhere. He wasn't *that* kind of lost this time.

Misdirected, maybe. Searching, yes. But not *lost* lost. *That* kind of lost implied something darker, something deeper.

Something in danger of never being found.

Looking into the teary eyes of the raccoon sent his mind sinking deep into the ache of it. Marcel remembered the exact way it felt.

The terrifying way his heart beat a hole in his chest when he realized what he'd done.

The panic that set in with every still-lost step.

The despair that mounted as afternoon turned to evening and evening turned to night.

And then the days, the weeks of walking the park, the city streets, and wishing he could take it all back.

Turning up in Mousekinland was like being one of those ships in movies, pushed a little off course.

It did not feel like being a ship lost at sea.

That was the worst kind of lost.

That day in the park. The backpack. Dorothy's warning. Marcel's wandering.

If it hadn't been for that *boy*! Ethan. The one that kept taking so much of Dorothy's time!

The soccer drills. Skateboarding. Partners for a science project and nights spent typing away into her phone.

It reminded Marcel of his first owner, Sweetie Jones. It had started with a few nights after work. Then it was every night that she was out late. Soon Sweetie hadn't any time to play with Marcel, clean his cage, or take care of him at all. Sweetie Jones had met a guy. And it just so happened that Sweetie's guy "wasn't a fan of animals." So she gave Marcel to her co-worker Ed. Ed who'd liked Marcel's spines.

Until he didn't.

If they'd just left the park five minutes sooner,

Ethan never would've come to ask Dorothy to play. If only Marcel hadn't gotten so worried, even jealous again. If not for *the bird, the bicycle basket, the basset hound,* things might've been so different.

But what was it the bird had said that day? Oh, yes.

She'd said that once you leave the nest, you can never go back.

And he had left. He'd made a decision and he'd gone. He'd never truly know if it was the right decision, but given the evidence . . . Well, he was something of an expert at reading the evidence, after all. All he knew was that if Dorothy was going to give him up like the rest, then he didn't want to be there when she did.

That day in the park, Marcel had been a ship.

Not a ship a little off course.

He'd been a ship without a radio, without a lighthouse, without a North Star to guide him—a ship lost at sea.

That's who Dorothy was. His North Star. The very thing that leads you home.

That's what being *lost* lost was.

It was losing your only way back.

"Ahem," whispered Scamp. "This seems to be taking a while. You *are* coming up with a plan, aren't you? Marcel?"

Marcel shook the memories from his head and the hurt from his heart. He nodded.

Focus, he told himself. He needed to focus. He needed to help this raccoon.

And who knows? Maybe the little guy wasn't really *lost* lost after all.

Maybe being found waited just a few trees away.

Marcel forced himself to smile. "We're looking for something too. Would you like to look together?" The raccoon blinked at him.

"It's just that it's getting a little dark. In the morning maybe? After a bit of supper?"

The raccoon didn't budge.

"I know what it's like to be lost," Marcel said finally. If he knew what it was like to be permanently and forever lost, well, he wasn't about to stand by and let this little tyke find out too. He could hear Dorothy's voice in his head as he told the raccoon, "I'll take care of you if you'll trust me—it only takes a little."

The raccoon seemed to consider this. He nodded slowly.

"Good," said Marcel, feeling a tiny bit relieved. "Come on."

The three travelers led the lost raccoon to their camp in the roots of the old oak. Marcel held his hand. Uncurled, the raccoon was larger than all of them. Much bigger than Marcel. Rounder than Ingot. And with his bottlebrush of a tail, longer than Scamp a dozen times over. Marcel supposed they must look a little silly leading him like they were.

They fed the youngster a dinner of acorns and a little corn Scamp had tucked in her pack and settled him into a bed of leaves in the tree roots. It was dark now, and the forest crackled and moaned around them. In the moonlight, under a thick blanket of pine boughs they'd covered themselves with, Marcel could see the raccoon's eyes were wide and following every sound.

Ingot's breath became heavy and Scamp's snore tore through the quiet like a train whistle. But the raccoon couldn't sleep.

Marcel tried to distract him. "Feeling better?"

The raccoon hesitated at first, but then nodded.

"Do you have a name?"

The raccoon looked at him, opened his mouth and then closed it.

"You know," said Marcel gently. "I can't exactly call you *little guy* forever. Friends know each other's names. And you've already met me." He picked up Toto. "And here's Toto. He's a cocoon right now—but he'll be something sensational in time."

The raccoon put out a timid hand and touched the cocoon, who wriggled a happy wriggle. The raccoon smiled and pointed to himself. "Tuffy," he whispered.

"You are tough! Very tough!" Marcel said encouragingly.

"No!" said the raccoon. "I'm not tough. I'm Tuffy!"

Marcel understood. "Your name . . . it's Tuffy?"

The raccoon nodded his head enthusiastically, and his furry ears wiggled.

"Tuffy, well," said Marcel. "That's a nice name. Uh . . ." While he had him talking, Marcel figured he better get to the important task of seeing what a toddler was doing this far out in woods and if he was truly lost, or just a little off course. "Tuffy, why were you all alone in that tree? Is your family nearby, you think?"

Tuffy got very small. His ears drooped. "Tuffy's all alone," he whispered.

Marcel tried not to sound dismayed. "But what about your parents?"

Tuffy seemed to brighten. "They're in the half-a-tree!"

"The half-a-tree?" Marcel wasn't sure he'd heard him right, but it sounded very hopeful. If Tuffy's parents lived in a tree, it was likely they were here in the forest, and likelier that they were nearby looking for him. Marcel smiled at the thought.

Tuffy grabbed a leaf and nibbled it into the shape of a tree with a large section of the tree's leaves and branches torn clean away. He held it out to Marcel.

"The *half-a-tree*—it's a tree shaped like this?" Marcel asked.

Tuffy nodded again. "The half-a-tree. By the eat-box!"

Oh dear, thought Marcel. What in the world was an eat-box?

"The half-a-tree by the eat-box. But don't touch the fire-wire. The fire-wire stings you. . . ."

A *fire-wire*?

"Stay away from the honkers! The honkers are squashing you up!"

Honkers, thought Marcel. *Maybe geese?* He sighed.

Half-a-trees, fire-wires, and honkers. Oh my.

But Tuffy was still talking. "I was in a honker. The honker brought Tuffy here—"

Definitely *not a goose.*

"—to the mean-trees. After the snap-trap ate him."

Marcel tried to put it all together. This he knew: Tuffy came here by honker after a snap-trap ate him; honkers were dangerous, as were fire-wires; and he'd lived near an eat-box in a tree with a large bite taken out of it. Marcel looked at the tree-shaped leaf again.

Something about the sharp cut of the tree jogged his memory. Marcel had seen trees like this. It was as if something had carved out a portion of the branches. Now, what could do such a thing? And *why*?

Then it hit him.

In the city. He'd seen trees like that on a few streets. Once, he saw a crew of men sawing away at an overgrown maple, making room for a too-close power line the tree had wrapped itself around.

Wait. A power line. *The fire-wire!*

"Tuffy! Do you live in the city?" Marcel asked excitedly.

"Yup. I live in the city—near the eat-box. People don't like it when Tuffys eat from their eat-boxes. They catch you in their snap-traps and throw you in their honkers and bring you to the mean-trees."

Marcel could picture it now. Tuffy's family lived in a tree in the city. They ate out of . . . not refrigerators—that would be too hard to get to. Maybe . . . garbage cans? Yes! That was it! Garbage cans. Or dumpsters! And someone set a trap and caught Tuffy in it and put him in a *honker*—a car or a truck?—and brought him to the mean-trees. *The forest!*

Marcel sat back, exhausted but relieved. He felt certain he'd figured it all out.

Tuffy looked up at him from his little crook in the roots and patted him. "Are you going to help Tuffy get home to his half-a-tree?"

It dawned on Marcel then. The little raccoon really *was* lost. *Really* lost.

Those city streets could be tricky, he knew. Without a clue like the theater's popcorn scent or a trail of some kind, those streets could spin you right around. Street after street, building after building, they blended together.

From his seat in Dorothy's bicycle basket, Marcel had never paid much attention. He'd just closed his eyes and let the wind breeze through his quills.

Faster, Marcel? Dorothy would say. *Want to be the first hedgehog to fly?*

Flying hedgehogs didn't need directions.

They raised their arms and soared.

He'd never paid attention, because he'd never imagined one day he'd be sloshing through those same gutters and sleeping under newspapers. Never imagined he'd be calling her name, trying to find her, hoping the bird was wrong and that even if you leave the nest, there's still a way to get home.

"You will help Tuffy?" the raccoon asked again.

Marcel looked at him and worked up a brave face. The raccoon didn't know how next to impossible his ask was.

And Marcel wasn't going to be the one to tell him.

They'd just have to try.

"Sure, that's what I'm going to do. I'm on my way to the city too," Marcel said. "We'll . . .

we'll find your family. We, um, just need to get through the rest of the woods first." He nodded in the direction of the deepest, darkest part of the woods, where the hemlocks crouched together and the pines were so deeply green they looked almost black. "Ingot says it's that way."

Tuffy's eyes popped wide, and he began to shiver. "Oh no. The mean-trees—"

"But that's the way," reassured Marcel. "I'll be with you. So will Scamp and Ingot."

The raccoon still trembled.

"What are you so scared about?" Marcel asked.

Tuffy ducked his head a little. He looked around nervously. He barely made a sound as he said, "Snatchers."

"Snatchers?"

Tuffy raised his arms and flapped. Twice. Then he looked at his hands and his little nails—and plunged them into his furry belly like claws.

Tuffy whispered, "Near the mean-trees. Tuffy was looking for an eat-box. Tuffy saw them." His eyes grew wide. "The snatchers. They were snatching up a chipper. They were taking him."

Tuffy grabbed hold of Marcel's hand. "Tuffy doesn't want to go back to the mean-trees. Tuffy . . . he's too scared."

And who could blame him.

For the next hour, Marcel worked to calm the raccoon. He told him stories. Wonderful stories. About the theater, the hens, anything that might make him smile, and waited for the raccoon to drift off to sleep.

But later, alone with his thoughts, Marcel had to admit he agreed with Tuffy. The mean-trees seemed like a place they'd want to avoid the next day. A place they might never come out of if they ventured inside . . .

Trees like a dark sea . . .

A sea a ship could lose itself upon.

He was up all night just thinking about it.

CHAPTER 12

Pick a Star

THERE ARE SUNRISES THAT MAKE ALL OTHERS pale in comparison. The next day's was just such a one. It came on blue and sparkling orange wings, and if you only looked to the horizon, the world seemed very alive, full of promise—like anything at all was possible.

Except getting a cowardly raccoon to move.

Though the group rose early, much of the morning was spent trying to convince Tuffy to make the trek through the deep woods.

Marcel coaxed and cajoled.

Scamp suggested bopping him over the head.

Toto was no help, as wiggling isn't exactly a call to courage.

In the end, it was Ingot who convinced the raccoon to leave. "I been through this wood now a thousand times, and never once did I do it without being afraid. But I know the way. I know how to get you there safe. Besides, you got a mushroom medal. Sometimes you just do things and you do them scared, and that's that."

It did the trick. (Marcel spotted Tuffy stroking his mushroom medal lovingly.)

After filling their sacks with the leftover acorns from breakfast, the travelers set out, Ingot in the lead. Tuffy ran up and grabbed hold of the old squirrel's hand, and Ingot made to wrench it away. But the raccoon's grip was firm. Tuffy gazed at Ingot with awed admiration.

"You, uh, got quite a grip there, kid," said Ingot. He looked to the others; his dark eyes seemed to plead with them.

"I'm not holding his hand," said Scamp. "He'd probably eat it or something."

Marcel pointed to Toto, strapped to his chest, and shrugged.

"Everyone's so anxious to get where they're going but can't lift a finger for the old squirrel over here," Ingot growled. "S'pose I'll be making you all dinner and tucking you in tonight too." He turned and pulled Tuffy after him, grumbling as he went. "Don't know how I got myself wrapped up in all this. I'm too old! Should've barred that tractor door."

The mean-trees, Marcel guessed, were a dense patch of ancient spruces, hemlocks, and firs gnarled with years and heavy with moss. The air here had a nip to it, and the light was dim. Thin wisps of fog curled between thick trunks of cedar and disappeared into forest deeper still. All was bleak evergreen, grim browns, and blackest black.

There was a hush to the forest. The trees, packed tight like matchsticks, seemed to steal even the slightest noise. Sound was swallowed up by their roots, bark, and branches, and the travelers hesitated to add even a whisper. When they did, it was mostly Ingot who said something like, "Watch the root here," or, "There's a slippery patch there." Even Scamp kept her comments bottled up, busying herself with collecting wild mushrooms for dinner and scanning the trees with beady eyes for signs of trouble.

A few times Marcel thought he heard whispers. He couldn't make out any clear words—only what sounded like *governor, governor*. But as he'd seen no trace of bird or butterfly, rabbit or rodent around these parts, he told himself it was only the sound of their feet in the peat moss.

(It made him feel a little better.)

When they got to an area where every tree looked the same and the canopy of pine fringe blocked out all but the weakest light, Ingot ran up one of the trees to get a better look.

"We'll get to the grove by nightfall, but just," he said when he came back down a minute later. He handed them ferns to cover themselves, to blend in. "Get a spring in your step now. And look lively. There's mischief about."

The day wore on. The air grew frostier.

"Smells like snow," Scamp murmured to herself. "Harvest's almost over."

Marcel thought again about what Scamp was missing back in Mousekinland. He turned to question her about this, but the look in Scamp's eye when she realized he'd heard her made him snap his mouth shut. He scrambled to catch up to Ingot, who was pulling Tuffy behind him.

But as they picked their way through the trees, Marcel's mind was stuck on Mousekinland. The hurried scrambling and storing of food. The percussive building—carts and mouse houses, the roofs of storage sheds and pantry doors—and the muffled digging of tunnels. The whole town had seemed frantic in their preparations. Had Marcel pulled Scamp away just when they needed her most? She'd tried to convince him it wasn't such a big deal, but he wondered. She'd been gone for days now.

Marcel stumbled over a twig and reached out to steady himself on the trunk of a fir. As he did, his eyes snagged on something off in the wood.

Two yellow balls appeared to glow in some bramble twenty yards away.

Were they flames? Were they *eyes*? Marcel grabbed his glasses off his nose, rubbed them against his belly, and popped them back on.

He saw nothing but the black maw of the forest.

Marcel blinked. He cleaned his spectacles again. He tried squinting.

There was nothing. Nothing at all.

He considered mentioning it, but then thought better of it. Tuffy had done well today (after they finally got him moving, that is). True, Ingot had complained once or five times about the raccoon trailing him with his eyes pinched shut, slow as a snail, but Tuffy *had* followed.

Still, those two perfectly round torches—*were* they eyes?

Surely it was only a trick of the light.

"Thought you said we'd get there by nightfall."

Scamp had lagged behind the others for the

last hour. Impatient with how long the ordeal was taking, she kept stopping to chew a dagger out of a nice piece of wood she'd found.

"I said I *thought* we'd get there by dark," Ingot grunted over his shoulder. "There was no telling I'd be dragging a raccoon the whole way and waiting for the rest of you to catch up." He ducked under a low-hanging branch and had to wait for Tuffy to climb through. "We're lucky the moon's out tonight. Least we got a lantern to see by."

Ingot had broken his cardinal rule. No traveling by night in the forest. But when they hadn't gotten to his desired stopping place by nightfall, he'd left them near a stump with orders to cover Tuffy's ears while he scrambled off to spout owl calls into the dark. When his calls went unreturned, he'd deemed it safe to keep going.

Beyond the treetops, the moon hung like a silver coin in the sky. On the forest floor, against the bark of the trees, and bouncing off the damp sheen of every rock, the light landed in tiny spatters. It was as if the stars had fallen into the western woods and hadn't yet flickered out.

And it made Marcel think of Dorothy.

He hadn't thought about Dorothy's stars in a long time. He hadn't let himself.

But once upon a time, on an unremarkable street . . .

Where birds twittered in birdbaths, hounds brayed behind windows, where neighbors rocked on porch swings cradling steaming cups of tea . . .

Inside a cheery clapboard house with a tall maple and a tire swing and a flap on the front door just the perfect size for a hedgehog . . .

In a cozy third-floor bedroom strung with fairy lights, paper lanterns, homemade garlands, and a few dirty socks . . .

There was a hidden universe of stars.

Every night, after Dorothy finished her homework or settled her bookmark in the pages of a book, she'd pull the plug to the fairy lights, snap off the lamp next to her bed, and in the space of three seconds—the time it took for Marcel's eyes to adjust—the room was plunged into outer space.

Hundreds of glowing bits of greenish light held fast to the ceiling in whips and whorls. They trailed down the walls, hunkered in corners, dotted the bookshelf, dresser, and chair. The gleam of a nebula clung to the closet door. Even the windows held traces of starlight.

Pick one, Marcel, Dorothy would say. *Pick a star.*

But there, from his cage, Marcel wouldn't—not yet. He'd wait for Dorothy to raise a freckled arm and point to some corner of the ceiling.

There, she'd say. *That one's mine.*

It was a different star every night. And once Marcel laid eyes on Dorothy's star, then and only then, would he choose his own. Not too close, but never too far. A star that could reach out and touch hers if only it tried. *That* would be Marcel's pick of the night. That would be his wishing star.

Because even in the heavens he never wanted to be more than a hairbreadth away from her. All he'd ever wanted was to be always by Dorothy's side.

Ingot piped up from the front of the group. "We're close now. I can smell the fruit trees."

"Huh?" Marcel heard Scamp say from pretty far behind.

They wound through a low channel of rock and ferns, and after finding a foothold, they climbed the mud-slick ridge back into the trees. The spaces between pine and fir widened, and the sky opened up in lacy patches overhead. Ahead, moonlight shone into a clearing just beyond a rim of hemlock.

Tuffy shivered and slowed his pace. Ingot turned and pulled, but now the raccoon wouldn't budge.

"What now? We made it through the thickest part of the woods—your mean-trees or whatever you call 'em. What's the matter now?" asked Ingot.

Tuffy threw his paws up over his masked eyes. "Those were not the mean-trees," he whispered, uncovering an eye and pointing to a group of squat trees in the clearing. "*Those* are the mean-trees. The scream-birds hide in the mean-trees! They watch with their yellow eyes. They are watching for the chippers and hoppers and Tuffys to eat their sweet-balls. Then they are screaming, and the mean-trees are throwing their sweet-balls at you, and the snatchers—"

"What's a snatcher?" puffed Scamp, finally catching up. "What's he talking about?"

"Keep going," Marcel told Tuffy. "Tell them about the snatchers."

"The snatchers are waiting." Tuffy's whisper was as small as could be. "To snatch the chippers away."

Scamp was aghast. "What do you mean? What's he mean?" She turned to Ingot and Marcel. "He said something about yellow eyes. Didn't he say something about yellow eyes?"

"The snatchers," said a frowning Ingot in a low voice.

Scamp had a strained look, like she was trying to piece things together. Instinctively, she reached for a weapon. "My sling-shooter!"

Scamp whirled around, groping at her belt and scanning the ground. "My sling-shooter's gone!"

"Probably set it down one of the hundred times you stopped to whittle that dagger of yours," said Ingot.

"We have to go back! I need my sling-shooter!"

Marcel, knowing just how helpful Scamp's sling-shooter could be, was about to agree, but Ingot was firm. "We're not traveling back, and that's final. You could've set it down hours ago! You don't even have"—he looked at Scamp's poorly chewed dagger—"you've got barely anything to protect yourself."

Scamp swallowed a sob. Her eyes brimmed with tears.

The squirrel was right, of course, but Scamp without her sling-shooter was like a bird without wings, a spider without legs, a hedgehog without eyeglasses. It wouldn't have surprised Marcel at all if she'd been born with it, cocked and ready to shoot.

Ingot gave Scamp an apologetic look before turning back to Tuffy. "Now, *what the hayseed* are sweet-balls?"

"Something you can eat, I guess," said Marcel. He thought a moment. "Didn't you say something a little while ago about fruit trees?"

"Fruit trees?" Scamp croaked. "Where?"

"Ahead," said Ingot. "The orchard next to the farmhouse."

"We're saved!" Scamp screeched. And she took off running.

"Scamp!" Ingot yelled after her. "Get back here! We can't be sure the field's safe!"

But Scamp was already past the stand of hemlock and racing into the glade beyond.

Ingot chased after her. Marcel grabbed Tuffy's hand, and they trailed as fast as they could until they reached the edge of the clearing.

Moonlight spilled like a white sheet over the open, overgrown grass, the crumbling outline of a long-abandoned stone farmhouse, and a small grove of apple trees. Everything was bleached and sparkling under a thick coat of frost.

Marcel unstrapped Toto from the leaf-sack on his chest and handed the cocoon to Ingot. He didn't like the thought of Scamp alone and unarmed out there. Not one single bit. "I'll go after her," he whispered to the others.

Marcel shook as he crept out into the grass,

scanning the sky, the field, the trees for possible danger. He walked faster. He broke into a run.

To the right a large group of seagulls roosted, asleep in the matted grass, a strange sight this deep in the forest. A rabbit, under the apple trees, dined quietly on the dropped fruit. Ahead, Scamp barreled toward the roofless farmhouse and the grass that had grown up around it like a fur rug.

As Marcel got closer, there seemed to be an assortment of items strewn about the house. A glass canning jar. An old soup pot. Wooden fruit crates and oil cans, holes poked in the sides and curtains fluttering in the breeze.

Curtains?

Windows and walkways. Doors and a great dining table. Marcel recognized it immediately.

A mouse village.

Between the stones of the foundation, the round entrances of a hundred tiny homes dotted the surface. A line of metal watering cans, each with the rusted-out hole of a door, squatted next to the remains of a wood pile with its own collection of little houses—homes that, from what Marcel could tell, sat abandoned. It was like another version of Mousekinland, a broken-down version, lifeless as the stones themselves.

High above, a twist of grass hung eerily from one of the house's eaves, and Marcel shivered.

Scamp picked her way through the tossed-about remains of the village, frost crunching under her feet. Near a broken waterspout in the house's crumbling foundation, she disappeared through a hole, and Marcel squeezed in after her. He soon found himself on a tilting stair landing, overlooking an open basement.

No roof covered the house, and much of the first floor had rotted away and lay open to the elements, the starry sky. Below, more of the mouse village lay thrown about, much of it floating on the ice of a shallow pool covering the cellar ground. Moonlight reflected off the surface.

Scamp scrambled down an overgrown grapevine to the bottom. Marcel could hear her banging and clanging below and marveled at how much noise one small mouse could make.

But then the noises stopped. Everything went silent. Marcel held his breath.

Scamp screamed.

"Scamp?" he called out.

Silence.

"Scamp?"

Nothing.

Marcel's heart beat violently, and he found himself looking up to the stars. Before he knew what he was doing, for the first time in a very long time, he picked one.

"Please let Scamp be okay," he pleaded. *"Please."*

The star twinkled back, cold and silent.

Marcel squeezed his eyes shut and looked away. *Scamp!*

Just then, a paw *thunk*ed over the edge of the landing.

Another followed, holding a familiar-looking sling-shooter.

"Told you we were saved!" Scamp shouted, pulling herself onto the landing and grinning wildly at

Marcel. "I always leave a few sling-shooters around. You never know when you'll need an extra."

"You lived here, then?" Marcel asked, trying to keep the shaking out of his voice. (Scamp was fine. It was better not to mention he was worried. Plus, he wasn't exactly ready for another one of Scamp's "I-can-handle-it" lectures.)

Scamp nodded. "I was born here." She disappeared back through the hole again, her voice echoing off the stones. "This was my favorite home, Marcel!"

"Then why'd you leave?" he asked.

Scamp's voice echoed back. "Oh, that. I, uh, accidently poisoned the water supply. But I can assure you, Marcel, it—"

A smile was tickling the corners of his mouth as Marcel squeezed in after her.

By now he had no trouble finishing *that* sentence.

"It wasn't your fault."

CHAPTER 13

The Sounds of Frost and Scream-Birds

IT TOOK COAXING, BUT MARCEL AND INGOT EVENTUally convinced Tuffy to cross the field (albeit with eyes closed) to the orchard, where they made camp for the night under an old fruit crate.

Sweet-balls, they found out, were apples, and from what they could tell, Tuffy had had a bad experience in this very orchard not long after he was caught in the snap-trap and brought to the woods and abandoned. But there was still something about scream-birds and snatchers they couldn't quite figure out.

"The mean-trees throw their sweet-balls at

you, and then the scream-birds and snatchers zoom you," Tuffy tried to explain with a mouth full of apple. Juice slipped down his whiskers and plopped on the grass.

Ingot leaned over and whispered to Marcel, "Think it's got anything to do with those seagulls in the field?"

"Could be," answered Marcel. "Gulls are sort of screamy."

"Flying *idiots*," Ingot growled. "Loud, obnoxious, fool-headed dolts with wings."

Marcel stiffened.

The Wizard of Oz had trees that threw apples, he remembered. *And* fool-headed flying things—the Wicked Witch's flying monkeys.

Neither of which were good situations to find yourself in.

The moon hovered overhead, and the three sat quietly, waiting for Scamp, who was out in search of a secret stash of seeds near an overturned wheelbarrow. They'd tried to talk her out of it, but she'd wielded her sling-shooter, told them she knew the land like the skin on her feet, and said if they tried to stop her, they'd be picking rocks out of their teeth.

They'd yielded.

Ingot piped up again. He had a dark look in his eye. "There's something else I don't like," he said. "Have you noticed how few animals we've come across? In the forest, but especially here in this field? Never used to be like that. Where are the mice, the moles, the chipmunks? As long as I've been alive, the field's where folks gathered. And now there's nothing but seagulls and a glimpse of a rabbit? Don't you think that's strange?"

"Maybe they're hiding," said Marcel.

Ingot grunted. "I think there's more to it than that."

That night, Marcel fell into a fitful sleep. Hens and Fruit Gems, sling-shooters and stars—they swirled through his waking and his dreams as the frost crackled outside. The frost sounded like:

Pick a star.

Pick a star.

Pick a star.

Pick a star. At first Marcel had. He'd wished every night. Those first few weeks after he'd lost Dorothy, he could hardly wait for dusk. Overcast skies broke his heart.

If he just picked the right one, he told himself. If he picked the right star, Dorothy's star, maybe his wish to go home would come true.

And so, every night, as soon as there was a good sprinkling of stars to choose from, Marcel had wished. Beneath a bush in the park, he'd wished. Sitting in a sewer grate filled with old sandwich wrappers and wads of chewing gum, he'd wished. Staring out a theater window.

The last time, he chose a particularly twinkly star and wished bigger and harder than he'd ever wished.

He was certain he'd picked the right star.

He'd spent all the next day on the roof.

He'd found his way to the roof not long after he'd arrived at the theater, while searching the entire place, top to bottom, for a peppermint his nose told him was there but could never find. Up a set of stairs and out the perpetually-propped-open door, the roof was a place Marcel would go to think, to dream. Sometimes he'd go to watch for a twister that might pluck him up and deposit him someplace else, just like in the movie. Watch for rainbows that might point him in the right direction. Watch for any glimpse of braids and red high-tops.

But that day on the roof, he knew. Dorothy would come to the theater. He could feel it.

He wanted to be the first to see.

He'd squinted down on the street, waiting.

Morning turned to afternoon. Clouds rolled in and evening settled.

Cars and trucks beeped by. On the sidewalk men strode in dark suits, umbrellas tucked under their arms. Women crossed the street toting briefcases, backpacks, chatting happily into phones and to babies in strollers. Kids raced one another on skates, scooters . . . and a skateboard.

Chock-chock-chock. Whizzzzzzzzzz.

He'd heard her before he'd seen her. Then the fuzzy flash of auburn braids.

Thrill and ache rose up in his heart together.

There she was! His Dorothy! Finally, after waiting and wishing for months, all those stars came through.

He'd shouted, "Dorothy! My Dorothy! I'm sorry! I'm here! Look up! Look up!"

Chock-chock-chock. Whizzzzzzzzzzz.

The skateboard flew down the sidewalk. Fast. Too fast.

She wasn't stopping. She wasn't coming inside!

Panic seized him. He raced back and forth on the concrete ledge of the roof. "Dorothy! My Dorothy!" he cried.

He couldn't jump. He couldn't climb down the air shaft in time. Hedgehogs do not fly.

His throat swelled up tight like a balloon. Tears stung his eyes.

His Dorothy.

She was going to pass him by.

At that moment, he spotted a bottle propped on the ledge a little way off, green and glinting.

He ran to it as Dorothy passed under the marquee.

Chock-chock-chock. Whizzzzzzzzzzzzzz.

He reached the bottle and tipped it over the edge just as Dorothy slowed near the end of the block.

The bottle sailed to the concrete and smashed.

Then Marcel saw two things at once:

Dorothy reaching the corner and turning out of sight.

And a man on a bike with screeching brakes and swerving tires, trying to avoid the glass on the sidewalk.

The man and the bike skidded into the street.

Spotting him, an enormous truck of clucking cages wrenched itself away and crashed into a streetlamp. Feathers flew.

But Marcel noticed none of that. Not the blustering of stopped traffic, nor the man, skinned-kneed but otherwise whole, explaining to two officers the bottle, the bike, the boisterous truck.

Marcel's ears, his eyes, his heart was fixed to the corner where Dorothy had disappeared. She was gone. Again.

He never wished on another star.

It wasn't that he'd vowed not to. And Auntie Hen's and Uncle Henrietta's arrival the following night certainly distracted him from a lot of things for a while. But that wasn't it either.

He just no longer believed. In wishes, in stars, in crazy hopes and impossible dreams.

But then tonight, in the old farmhouse, out of nowhere, he'd made a wish. It just happened.

And that wish came true. Scamp was okay.

Marcel curled into a ball.

Life, he supposed, was full of coincidences like that.

Marcel rolled over, and Scamp's howl pierced the night.

"Move over, you thistle-head! You stabbed me!"

Ingot startled out of sleep.

Tuffy woke and went immediately into a fit of frightened sobbing.

And by the time they all settled down again, Marcel was wide awake.

Lying on his back under the fruit crate, Marcel found himself with a perfect view of one star. The brightest, twinkliest star in the sky.

Pick a star, the frost said.

Remembering that day on the roof, remembering their last day in the park, Marcel couldn't bring himself to utter a thing.

Life was full of coincidences.

It was also full of facts.

The boy, the bird, the bicycle basket, the basset hound.

The fact that that *boy* had convinced Dorothy to leave Marcel alone under the tree, just like he'd gotten her to stay after school, skateboard to the pizza shop, sign up for a week away at soccer camp.

The fact that the *bird* was right about being increasingly left alone. More and more.

"They stop coming back so often," the bird had said. "First they're there all the time—bringing you food, keeping you warm. But something in the wind changes."

It was at that moment that a breeze had blown through, and Marcel shivered as he watched Dorothy practice soccer drills out on the lawn with Ethan. And the bird, watching her parents soar on the breezes above her, went on, affirming his every fear.

"They stop coming back so often. Then they push you from the nest. Then you spend the next few weeks on the ground, hiding under bushes, fighting with worms, and hoping nothing eats you."

She'd looked from where Marcel sat on the ground in Dorothy's backpack to the bicycle and its basket, propped against the tree. "That your nest there?" she'd asked about the basket—Marcel's basket.

The *bicycle basket.* He'd seen it with his own two eyes. He couldn't deny the fact of that sign there. Those two small words.

Those two words said it all. And wasn't it only a matter of time before Dorothy got tired of him like all the others? Surely he'd been right, hadn't he?

But even if he somehow got it all wrong . . .

Once you leave the nest, you can never go back.

Marcel now took one last look at the star before curling up in a ball.

"I wish," he whispered to himself. "I wish for clouds."

✦ ✦ ✦

They were all feeling a bit surly the next morning.

Well, maybe except for Scamp. She'd already disappeared on one of her mousely errands.

"Left before I woke," Ingot told Marcel. "Never heard a peep. Too tired. Don't take well to folks being speared in the middle of the night." He aimed a pointed glare at Marcel as he said this.

While they waited for Scamp's return, the three travelers munched on a few spongy apples they'd collected the night before. But when Scamp took longer than expected, they decided someone should get a look around. They drew blades of grass. (They made sure Tuffy's was longest.) Marcel pulled the short one.

He was only halfway out of the crate, when

a barrage of rotting apples pummeled him.

Thwoop-thwoop-thwoop-thwoop. Slllllllllurp. A mashed apple slopped off the crate.

The squalls of a hundred seagulls filled the air.

"Scream-birds!" cried Tuffy, falling to the ground and covering his ears.

"Great," snarled Ingot.

Marcel's surprise turned to worry. Where was Scamp?

He looked to Ingot. "What do you think they want?"

The gray squirrel was fuming. "*Want*? How should I know! They're flighty, unpredictable. *Flying idiots.*" He scowled. "Better leave it to me. Here's what we do: you lift the crate enough for me to slip out, and I'll lead them out into the front field. The two of you can sneak out the far side of the orchard and head for the forest yonder."

Tuffy shook his head fiercely. "Oh no, oh no, the mean-trees hit you with their sweet-balls and the scream-birds—"

"Don't be worrying your fuzz-brain about

sweet-balls," grumped Ingot, but at the same time, he patted the raccoon with a tender hand. "I'll be halfway out of the mean-trees before your scream-birds even know what's happened. Just do as I say. I've dealt with these blockheads before."

This didn't feel right to Marcel. Scamp was missing again, there were a hundred squalling birds just outside, and now Ingot was going to try to lead the gulls away? He looked to a quivering Tuffy who dove to the ground and used his tail to cover his eyes.

Hmm.

If they had any hope of getting the raccoon out of this fruit crate, this was as good a plan as any.

"Are you sure you can outrun them?" Marcel asked Ingot as the squirrel prepared himself for his dash by stretching his legs a bit.

"I got it, Spike" was all Ingot said, but they exchanged worried glances. "Let's go."

On the count of three, Marcel and a persuaded Tuffy lifted the crate a few inches off the grass, and Ingot dashed out and sprinted for the field.

Apples exploded on the ground around the wooden crate. The flapping of wings and the awful screeching of the flock filled the air.

"Wait," Marcel told Tuffy. "When it starts to get quiet, we'll know it's safe to run."

Sure enough, the sound of screeching became distant, leaving Tuffy's worried breathing the loudest sound in the orchard.

"They've followed him, Tuffy," said Marcel. "Time to go."

The raccoon backed into the corner, covered up his mushroom medal, and shook his head. "Tuffy wants to stay," he whispered shakily.

"Tuffy, you can't—Ingot's led them away. We've got one chance to make a break for it!"

The little raccoon sat his furry bottom on the ground with a *thump*. "Tuffy is scared. I'm the scarediest Tuffy in the world."

"Look," said Marcel as a thought came to him. He propped up the crate and stepped outside.

Not one of Tuffy's sweet-balls burst onto the scene.

"See?" Marcel cried. "It's safe! Have a look! No apples!"

A black eyeball peeked through a crack, but the raccoon made no effort to come out.

The screaming of the gulls was still a way off, but all at once there came a loud, triumphant chorus of caws. Marcel whirled around to spot the flock.

Off in the middle of the field, the sea of birds gathered in a melee of white wings; a cloud of gulls boiled overhead. A few broke away from the pack and began to fly back toward the orchard.

"Tuffy!" shouted Marcel. "They're coming back! We have to leave! *Now!*"

Tuffy let out a sob. Then a hiccup.

"Now!" Marcel shouted again as he turned over the crate and tried to push Tuffy into action. The raccoon wouldn't move a muscle.

Marcel aimed his barbs. "Sometimes what you need is a little nudge," he heard himself say, and at that, he needled the raccoon with a generous *BOINK* of his spines.

Tuffy jumped a foot into the air.

And now that he was moving, Tuffy ran.

The two weaved through the apple trees and around the overturned wheelbarrow, trying not to slip on the hundreds of rotting apples that lay scattered everywhere like small, wilted balloons. Marcel kept watch for any sign of Scamp.

Breaking through the edge of the orchard, Marcel could hear the cawing of the gulls behind him but knew he hadn't a moment to look. His eyeglasses threatened to bounce off his nose as he raced through the back field, and he tore them off. He clutched them now between his teeth as he raced past the raccoon. "This way, Tuffy!"

The forest's trees grew steadily higher as Marcel and Tuffy got closer. Marcel's weak eyes couldn't make out more than a black mountain of pine. "We're almost there," he shouted to Tuffy behind him. "We'll make it!"

But then, like the lowering of a theater curtain, a white sheet fell slowly before them. Marcel slowed. He threw his glasses back onto his nose.

He stopped fast.

Tuffy tumbled into him from behind and yelped at the poke of Marcel's spines as the two went rolling and came to a stop.

Marcel lifted himself from the meadow floor.

The last of the curtain of gulls dropped, blocking their way to the forest.

Before them sat an army.

Ingot was nowhere in sight.

CHAPTER 14

Off to See a Whizzer

A FINAL BIRD FLEW DOWN AND LANDED BEFORE them. He cocked his head to the side and stared at Marcel intently.

"What do you have there? On your face."

Marcel reached up and touched his glasses. "They're—" he stammered. "They're so I can see."

The seagull cocked his head again. "Do they taste good?"

Marcel stopped shivering. "Why—why no. They aren't something you eat."

"Too bad," said the seagull. He turned to the flock. "Too bad, isn't it?"

A thousand *yeses, affirmatives,* and *too bads,* rose up from the sea of birds behind him.

The lone seagull faced Marcel and Tuffy again. "Too bad indeed."

Marcel stepped forward. "I'm Marcel. And this is my friend Tuffy. We'd like to get by ,if you don't mind. We won't be any trouble."

The seagull looked sharply from Marcel's feet to where he'd first stood and then back again. Marcel scooted back.

The seagull narrowed his eyes and grinned. "You won't be going anywhere, my pointy friend—at least not without assistance."

Marcel gulped. Tuffy's eyes were wide, his hair mussed. He whimpered.

Marcel tried another approach. He shifted his leaf sack and lifted a tiny hedgehog claw. "You know, if you're hungry, I have a few candies here—"

"Did I ask you to speak?" snapped the seagull. He turned to his comrades. "Did I say he could speak?"

A chorus of *nos, negatives,* and *I-don't-think-sos* erupted from the field.

Marcel wrung his paws. Tuffy looked as if he might faint.

"Enough," said the seagull. "Bring the squirrel here."

At the lift of his wing, three gulls rose from the orchard carrying familiar cargo beneath them. One on each arm and another gull with Ingot's bushy tail clutched in its claws, they flew across the field and dropped the squirrel between the two sides with a *thump*.

A sheepish and unsteady Ingot stood, brushed himself off, and with a bit of a limp, plodded over to Marcel and Tuffy. "Seems I'm not as limber as I thought."

Ingot looked thin and small to Marcel. Older by at least a decade. Whether it was the nights of poor sleep or his recent clash with the gulls, had he looked this way a few minutes ago, Marcel would never have agreed to let him go in the first place. He was, Marcel saw now, patently ancient.

"That's right," said the seagull in an oily voice. "Go ahead and join your little friends."

Ingot turned on him. "You're a long way from the river, Monk!" he shouted, and the sound of him, barbarous and strong, made up for any deficit of appearance. "What do you want with us? And since when is it a crime to cross this field?"

"Since we've instituted a price—a price *you* haven't paid," snapped the gull.

It was clear this wasn't the first time the two had met.

Ingot laughed bitterly. "I've crossed this field more times than you can count. This here's open ground since the farmer left. Mice, moles, chipmunks, rabbits, squirrels—all have gotten on just fine living here, crossing here, without any price to pay."

"Things change," Monk answered. "Besides, you haven't been around in . . . what? How many years now?"

Ingot's eyes went dark. "That's none of your business," he growled.

"It is when you try to cross my field," said the seagull.

The graying sky turned bleaker, and a chilly wind blew across the meadow, kicking up leaves. A few spun into the wide, gaping sky, and the seagull army puffed out their feathers and hunched against the cold.

Monk and Ingot were locked in an icy glare until the seagull's eyes melted at the corners and he smiled a wicked smile. "I remember, you know. A seagull doesn't forget," he said. "I remember what you lost. A wife. A boy and girl—"

Marcel sucked in his breath.

"Enough!" shouted Ingot.

"Touchy, aren't we, Governor?"

Governor! The whispers in the forest. So Marcel *had* heard right!

The seagull strode up to Ingot, inches from his nose. "Come now, old friend. You and me—we can make a deal. We could use you around these parts again. I'll even see to it your companions here are safe. You don't want to lose anything more to the *witch.*"

Marcel sucked in his breath. He didn't like the

look in the seagull's eyes. He didn't like the way Ingot's shoulders slumped when Monk mentioned a wife. A boy and girl. Had Ingot lost them to . . . *the witch*? To Wickedwing?

The frost sounded like broken glass under his feet as Marcel took a timid step forward. He stammered. "M—my friends and I, we're happy to pay a fair price, if this is your field, sir. We've got a few acorns left over, and we can get mushrooms—"

Ingot pushed him away. "Ignore the hedgehog. We pay nothing. You will let us cross."

At this, the sea of birds lifted their heads and began to screech and caw, their wings flapping in quick, excited movements.

Monk stepped closer and smiled menacingly at the threesome, but it was to Ingot he spoke. "I know it's hard to understand, as it's been a while since you've graced this part of the forest with your presence, Governor. But you gave up any voice you might have had a long time ago. Don't blame you. You did lose a lot. What reason was there to stay? But there's an understanding now. Between me, the witch, and Whizzer."

Marcel noticed a look of confusion cross Ingot's face. He wondered if it had to do with whoever this Whizzer was.

"The boundary lines have been set," said the seagull. "She's got a few rules. Whizzer's got his stores. The fields? They're *mine*." The words came out biting. "Trespassers *will* pay. If you're incredibly lucky, maybe more than one of you will be spared. But you *will* pay."

"What happened to the animals in these parts?" demanded Ingot. The fur at the back of his neck stood up. "What did you do to them?"

At the mention of missing animals, Marcel scanned the field for any sign of Scamp.

The mouse had disappeared into thin air.

"Animals?" The gull gave his attempt at a confused look. He turned to his comrades. "Anybody remember any animals 'round these parts?"

The contingent of birds threw up another round of raucous squalls.

"You've got bigger things to worry about than

a bunch of mice and moles." Monk took a step closer, and every gull in the field followed suit. "How about we take little trip to see *Whizzer*."

Zing.

Something small shot past the gull's face and sank into the ground.

"What in the—"

Zing! Zing! Zing!

Three more bullets rained down into the flock of agitated birds. Their wings poked up. The field was astir, the seagulls' cries growing with every shot.

"What's going on? Where's it coming from?" shouted Monk, spinning around and scanning the field, the trees behind him.

Zing! Snap!

A pained cry went up from a gull near the back. Four gulls nearby flew into the air and began to head over the treetops.

"The farmer!" squawked one.

"His shotgun!"

"He's come back!"

"My wing—oh, my wing!" shouted the gull near the rear. "I've been *hit*!"

The screaming of the gulls grew so loud, Marcel, Ingot, and Tuffy were forced to cover their ears.

Three more gulls took off over the trees. The remaining birds were in chaos.

"Where are you going?" screeched Monk. His neck was thrust out, his wings up, and his cold, yellow eyes were wide with fury. "Get back here!"

Zing! Zing! Zing! Snap!

A bullet hit its mark. It struck with such force, the leader of the gulls fell to the grass.

The gulls screamed their terrible screams. First ten, then twenty, then fifty took to the air in search of safety.

Monk rose to his feet. A few feathers on one side bore a trickle of blood. He stumbled. Twenty more gulls disappeared over the dark forest.

"You," snarled the seagull. "You *will* pay." After a last poisonous look, he took a step toward the trees, and then another. A disordered run followed, and soon he lifted off and into the wind.

The rest of the pack—what was left of it—followed, and in moments Marcel and the others couldn't tell gray sky from gull as the last of them hastened over the treetops.

Quickly, Ingot limped over the frosty grass and grabbed Tuffy's arm. "To the trees now! Quick as you can! They'll be back as soon as they figure out it wasn't the farmer!"

Marcel stole a glance at the wide-eyed Tuffy, but he was relieved to see him obey, his fear of scream-birds seemingly greater than that of the forest.

"I'll bring up the rear!" shouted Ingot. "You two fly! Make for the trees! Keep your eyes to the ground—I'll watch the sky! Now go!"

They flew across the open field and into the thicket at the forest's edge. A maze of wild black-berry, ivy, and thorns tugged at them as they went. Deeper. Deeper still.

Ingot was puffing when he finally caught up. "We stick to this bramble where we can, so they can't see us. Not sure they'd venture in anyway, with all that talk of boundaries . . ."

Tuffy tugged at Ingot's hand and wiggled his ears, a worn-out but relieved look in his eye.

"Yes, yes," Ingot said to him, and gave him a pat. "You did fine. You did just fine."

Tuffy smiled a little smile and adjusted his mushroom medal. "I did just fine," he whispered to himself.

The threesome stopped to catch their breath in a bit of bramble at the bottom of a large tree. Ingot flopped on his back, sprawled out and wheezing, as Tuffy curled up next to him.

"Just need to get my bearings," Ingot was saying. "It's been a while. Seems a lot has grown up in this part of the forest. Need a jog to the memory, that's all."

"What about Scamp?"

They'd made it past the seagulls, but Marcel still hadn't breathed. Scamp was still out there, and if anything had happened to her, he'd never be able to forgive himself. "We've got to go back to the farmhouse! What if the seagulls find Scamp?" he said, pausing to pluck a thorn from his fur.

"I wouldn't worry your prickly little head about a thing like that," said Ingot.

"We can't just leave her—she's our friend. She's the *Scarecrow*!" Marcel blurted out.

"*Scarecrow?* Don't know what the hayseed you're talking about," said Ingot. "But she's fine."

"How do you know?" demanded Marcel.

The squirrel shot him a disinterested look. "Because."

"Because why?"

Zing! Thwap! A single pebble lodged in the crumbling bark of the tree.

"Because *that.*" Not taking his eyes off Marcel, Ingot pointed a claw directly above them.

Marcel lifted his eyes.

Scamp, balancing on a branch a hundred feet in the air, dangled her sling-shooter from a paw.

Of course. How silly of him.

The little mouse tipped back her head and crowed.

"Scarlet 'Scamp' Mousekin, at your service!"

CHAPTER 15

Lost, Lost, All Is Lost

FOUR (AND A COCOON) ONCE MORE, THEY TRAVeled into the woods, single file. Ingot led, and as she was the only one with a weapon, Scamp insisted she was the natural choice for rear guard.

Marcel trudged along, deep in thought.

The fact they hadn't again come across the popcorn scent concerned him. How many days was it since he'd left the hens in the theater?

Five. Five days.

Marcel felt queasy.

But the right path would show itself, wouldn't it?

Worry began to eat at his nerves.

He worried about Auntie Hen and Uncle Henrietta.

He worried about Scamp. They were farther from Mousekinland than ever. How on earth would she get back on her own safely?

Ingot too. He was hurt. And as he limped along, Marcel realized there was now Monk's story to consider. It seemed Ingot had every reason not to join them on this journey.

And then there was all that talk of boundaries and witches and Whizzers.

It was the hens and Tuffy's need to get back to the city that kept him going. There was no point in splitting up the gang now. They were safer together.

He'd figure out how to do right by Scamp and Ingot later.

The going was slow. The forest twisted and turned at will. Several times Ingot had to stop to run up a tree and take stock of his surroundings, but the clouds hung low and he couldn't see past more than a few treetops. Once, they were forced to turn around when they came to a ravine too steep to climb. The four ducked under the low-hanging branches of every spiny and thorn-riddled tree and scrambled over roots thick as jungle snakes. They slogged around murky swamps rimmed in the blackest mud, swamps that looked ready to catch some weary traveler by a foot and pull them under for the rest of time.

After they'd tramped around their fourth such swamp, Scamp gave a startled cry from the rear.

"Look!" She pointed an accusing finger at the muck beneath her. "Oh, *scat in my hat*, you've led us the wrong way, Ingot! Our footprints are right there! We've already gone around this swamp!"

Sure enough, four sets of footprints oozed out of the mud.

"I—I was sure it was a left at the knotty pine," said Ingot. He scratched his head. His eyebrows knit themselves together. "It's been a while. But I was sure—"

"We are lost!" wailed Scamp. She threw down her

sling-shooter into the mud. "Lost, lost, all is lost!"

Ingot frowned deeper. "Well, that's a bit dramatic."

The little mouse stomped up to the squirrel, fists clenched into tiny knots, and glared at him. "*You* said you knew the way. I followed *you* because you said you knew how to get me and Marcel to the Emerald City Theater!"

Ingot squared his shoulders. "I did no such thing, missy. You were the one with all the promises. I said I'd help get you through the forest—that's it. And *that's* what I'm doing."

Scamp turned on her heel. "Could've fooled me," she snapped.

Scamp snatched up her sling-shooter and stomped into the trees. After a moment, she came back, eyebrows up and a look of annoyance on her face. "Well? You coming?"

Tuffy's eyes drifted from the mouse to Ingot and back to Scamp.

"Come on, Tuffy. Let's go," Scamp ordered.

Tuffy gave Ingot a sorrowful look and stepped toward Scamp. "I am coming."

"Marcel?" Scamp tapped her foot impatiently.

Marcel shifted. He bit his lip. He felt sorry for Ingot.

But the old squirrel seemed to understand. "It's okay, kid. We'll follow her for a bit. It'll give me time to figure things out. Just don't know how I got so mixed up. The old sniffer doesn't work the way it used to, I guess."

They trudged on. Scamp, now in the lead, was explaining to Tuffy her *particular* skills in sensing direction and avoiding ravines. "I knew it! I knew we were lost! But nobody thinks to ask the smallest mouse!"

She prattled on and on about mouse noses and noggins and her need of a sword. She was becoming, well, to be honest?

Insufferable.

Tuffy covered his ears.

Marcel hummed show tunes to drown out the sound of her voice.

Ingot stuffed a mushroom in each ear and looked almost blissful a second later.

"Just needed to use the old mouse-sense. It never lies!" Scamp was saying. "Your Emerald City is on the other side of these woods here, Marcel. I'd bet my sling-shooter on it."

Scamp was pretty fond of her sling-shooter, so the odds, Marcel felt, might be in their favor.

Marcel hung toward the back and the limping squirrel. He saw Ingot pop the mushrooms out of his ears and heard them disappear into the mud with a burp.

"I've never wished for the loss of hearing more," Ingot grumbled. "I just can't figure out how I got so turned around!"

Marcel tried to be reassuring. "I think anyone could lose their way in these woods. I don't think I've ever seen so many vines. Every tree looks exactly the same."

"Hrmph," said Ingot. "It would. When was the last time you been in a forest?"

Marcel frowned. "Well, nothing ever this big, but—"

"That's the thing about the woods," Ingot

interrupted. "You think you're on the right path, but the trees have their way with you. Too often it's not until you find your way out that you realize the path was right enough."

The right path. Marcel hopped over a patch of moss that squished under his feet and stopped on the other side to wipe them off on a few dried leaves. Hadn't he just told himself the right path would show itself?

But no.

The problem with that, he now realized, was that there could be a million paths, a million wandering streets, and sometimes . . .

You have a little too much trouble finding your way back, thought Marcel.

And that's why he'd taken precautions. That's why he'd made sure there was a path back for Scamp and Ingot. Yes. At least there was that.

Ingot stopped and stretched his back, and Marcel noticed him wince.

"I'm sorry," Marcel said. "For all of this. I'm sorry I dragged you here."

Ingot shook his head. "Sometimes a good dragging's what you need to get beyond your four walls."

"Was it Wickedwing?" Marcel blurted. "Was it the owl that did this to you?"

"Sheer bad luck did this to me," Ingot said, rubbing at his eyes. "Life did this to me. Life gives you things and takes them away. That's how it goes."

Up ahead, Scamp was going on about her uncanny ability to see pictures in the stars.

"I'll show you, Tuffy. There's a swan up there, and a duck with a tiny head. There's also two of my sling-shooters, a big one and a little one." She stopped and looked up past the pines, where the sky was still a thick blanket of cloud. "If the sun ever comes out again, I'll show you my favorite star. Maybe I'll even find *you* in the sky, Tuffy."

They'd trekked only a few seconds more before Scamp froze. "Oh no."

"What's that?" grunted Ingot.

Scamp's back was turned to them, and Marcel went to her. Scamp's eyes were fixed to the ground in front of her.

Four sets of tracks were pressed into the dirt. One mouse, one raccoon, one squirrel, and one hedgehog.

"It was Tuffy!" she explained. "I was distracted! I'm—I'm not lost. I just wasn't paying attention is all!"

Ingot hobbled to the front, and the four travelers stood in a small circle, staring down at the tracks.

"What now?" asked Marcel.

"But we were headed north," said Scamp. "I *know* we were going nor—"

"Haven't been headed north for some time," interrupted Ingot. "Look at the trees. The lichen—it grows on the northern side." He pointed to a nearby trunk with an icy-green coat. It mocked Scamp, and she swallowed hard.

Ingot sighed and shook his head. "We're taking a break," he said. "There's no sense going on if we can't make heads or tails of the way."

"No," said Scamp. "I'll find it. Just give me a min—"

Everyone startled as Ingot hammered a foot into the soft ground. "I am not just thinking about myself here, girl!" he thundered. "Marching through the forest without a notion to go on is not a walk in the park! If we continue, we run the risk of being miles from this city of yours! And if we run into trouble after dark—well, I've had enough excitement!"

Marcel winced. Ingot didn't know how nightmarish a walk in the park could actually be. The wailing wind and wild animals were one thing. But nothing's worse than thinking you've lost the one thing you love most. And nothing's scarier . . .

Than wondering if maybe it had all been a mistake.

"Just can't figure it out," Ingot went on. "All this talk of boundaries. Monk talking like the field's his. And Wickedwing's where? Who this Whizzer is, is anyone's guess! I don't like it. But what I do know is where we're standing now *isn't* our territory, and if we get caught like we were earlier, I fear the outcome won't be the same!"

Scamp was ready for a fight. "*Wickedwing, Wickedwing, Wickedwing!* I'm so sick of her and everything else! I'm sick of running! Sick of moving! Sick of everyone being so scared all the time! Look at us! We've been so afraid of that old witch, and have we gotten even a glimpse of her? NO! She's probably moved on! Probably miles down the river and never coming back! That night in the cornfield? I bet it was that old hawk we saw during the day! *Wickedwing—*" She spat on the ground.

"Don't tempt fate, Mouse. Just because you can't look evil in the eye doesn't mean it isn't there."

"I know that," snapped Scamp. "I know it more than *you*! I lived in that orchard too. I know all about the owl! I know things you don't!"

"Doubtful!" Ingot spat back. "I was governor of these parts before your daddy's granddaddy's granddaddy was even born! That field? I looked out for it!"

Ingot went on.

"I knew everyone and everything that went on, and now there's nothing, no one! I've seen what that owl can do, and I'll tell you what happened. What happened is she's hunted that field until there wasn't anyone left to hunt, and she's just waiting till she gets hungry enough to come looking for us! You and your big ideas. Head so big you'd probably trot right out if she knocked on your door! Young and *foolish*—"

"And you're a mean, fuzz-ball fossil! And *scared*!" Scamp's whiskers stood on end and she clawed at her cheek and neck. "And I am not foolish! I'm small, but I'm not dumb! What do you think I was doing while you all were sleeping under that fruit crate in the orchard! I was collecting information! The rabbit—she said it's the seagulls who're carting animals away! Why do you think they're there anyway? Besides, Wickedwing would've never let them sleep out in the open like that!"

Scamp narrowed her eyes at the old squirrel. "Shows what you know, you old bristle-tail. Most folks left before that anyway. The mice did. And seems everyone else did too, after I—"

Scamp instantly bit off her words, and her eyes grew wide. "I . . . I . . ."

"You what?" shouted Ingot.

"I . . . I—"

"Spit it out, girl!"

Scamp flopped onto the ground, covered her head, and began to wail. "I didn't mean to! I was only using it for target practice! And anyway, no one told me the box on the side of the well was rat poison! Who leaves rat poison just sitting there anyway?"

Ingot leaned over to Marcel. "What's she talking about?"

"She poisoned the water supply," Marcel explained. "It wasn't her fault."

Ingot's head drooped. He looked very tired all of a sudden. "I'm sorry. I got carried away again. I didn't know, kid. I never should have said those things. I—"

"Don't worry," Scamp said, and stood. Her eyes were red and puffy. "I'm used to it. You get used to people thinking you're stupid and reckless and wild and blaming you for everything. For being the reason the whole town had to leave and find another place—again. I'm used to people looking down on me. You're not special." She wiped her nose with an arm. "And by the way, the poison didn't hurt anybody. Old Mrs. Sniffers acted a little strange after she took a few sips of that poison water, but she was always a little weird."

"I think none of those things. I'm—I'm sorry. I spoke harshly," said Ingot. He rubbed his forehead. "Maybe we need a little break."

Scamp stomped over and disappeared behind a rock. "Just leave me alone," she said quietly.

Ingot stared off in Scamp's direction. He sat, leaned against a tree, and closed his eyes.

Marcel looked down at his feet. He patted Tuffy's hand. And then he did what he always did when he didn't really know what to do.

He got a snack.

Marcel led Tuffy off, and together they rounded up a few rubbery mushrooms. Tuffy found a walnut. Marcel plucked four shriveled blackberries from a wild vine, and though they weren't perfect, he could smell some juice in them still.

One for Scamp. One for Ingot. One for Tuffy. And one for him.

It felt a little hopeful.

The air grew colder as he and Tuffy searched, and a wind kicked up. The bones of the trees creaked and groaned, and Marcel checked to make sure Tuffy wasn't frightened.

The tyke stood a little way off, a large tear slipping down his face.

"Tuffy wants to be going home. I'm tired of the sad-trees."

"Oh, Tuffy." Marcel sighed.

The two of them settled under a tree with trailing branches like a curtain. It was like one of Dorothy's forts, Marcel realized. Her forts had been his favorite.

They always had plenty of snacks.

Marcel had a thought. "Would you like to see what's in my pack? I bet you can't guess."

Three Fruit Gems were all that remained.

Marcel pulled one out. Tuffy's ears wiggled, but he did not smile. Marcel broke off a piece and handed it to him. "Try it; it's good," he said.

Tuffy sat holding the candy in his lap . . .

And looking as dismal as a bucket of spilled popcorn in an empty theater.

Spilled popcorn.

The memory blew in like a breeze.

It was a few weeks after Dorothy had been spending more and more time away from Marcel. Planning a science project after school. Meeting friends at the mall. Even when Marcel and Dorothy were together, she'd been a bit distracted. Always fiddling with her phone. Chatting about school and books and boys. *The* boy. Ethan.

At first Marcel had used the time to get some exercise—taking laps around her room, tunneling through the laundry piled on the floor, pushing around the miniature soccer ball he'd found under the bed.

But after time, Marcel began to feel hurt. Weren't they *Lady and the Tramp*? *Fred Astaire and*

Ginger Rogers? Batman and Robin—the dynamic duo? Had something changed? Didn't Dorothy want to spend time with him anymore? Had he been replaced?

And then, after a long week of play practices and very few belly rubs, Dorothy came into the room with a big bowl of popcorn, and Marcel's heart soared.

She hadn't forgotten him! They'd curl up in a pillow fort and share their favorite snack. Marcel wondered what movie they'd watch. It didn't matter, of course, but he hoped Dorothy would choose their favorite, *The Wizard of Oz*.

But that's not what happened. Dorothy settled the bowl on the edge of the desk, pulled out some homework, and got to work. Here and there she reached over for a handful of popcorn.

She didn't offer him any.

Popcorn. Butter. Parmesan cheeeeeeese. They called to him. His belly was hungry, but his heart was hungrier.

Sadness, frustration, even anger bubbled up

inside him. He put one paw in front of the other, climbed his tunnel to the top of the desk, and ran to the bowl.

Even later he could never tell how much had been accidental and what was on purpose, but what happened next was the bowl toppled over the edge and landed facedown in his litter box.

Marcel stared at it, stunned. Dorothy did too.

What had he done?

He'd acted as brainless as a scarecrow, as heartless as a tin man, as cowardly as a lion afraid of *everything*. And then instinct took over and Marcel popped into a ball and shook.

He felt Dorothy's hands pick him up. She brought him close to her face.

"Oh, Marcel. I'm so sorry."

Marcel popped out of his ball. Dorothy kissed him on the nose. "I'll be right back," she said, depositing him on the bed.

And when she came back?

She was carrying the biggest bowl of popcorn he'd ever seen.

"I made enough for us both," Dorothy had said, licking Parmesan off a finger.

She said it like nothing in the world. Like he hadn't just spilled her popcorn. Like there was nothing to forgive.

And that's when Marcel knew.

That through the ups and the downs, whether near or far, that no matter what happened—

He'd spend the rest of his life hopelessly in love with her.

Love isn't always some grand, romantic thing, like in the movies.

Sometimes it's a kind gesture, forgiveness . . . a second bowl of popcorn.

Marcel swallowed hard. Maybe he *had* made a mistake. Maybe Dorothy had never stopped loving him. Maybe she loved him the exact same way he loved her! Maybe he'd run away for nothing.

Marcel shook his head firmly.

The boy, the bird, the bicycle basket, the basset hound.

The *boy* who'd stolen Dorothy's heart.

The *bird* who was right. Hadn't Marcel been

through it before with Sweetie Jones? The more and more they spend time away, the sooner they give you up, or . . .

They post a sign.

The *bicycle basket.*

"That your nest there?" the bird had asked. And it was, in a way. The wicker basket on Dorothy's bicycle was what he traveled in whenever Dorothy brought him along for the ride. But looking up at it then, he'd noticed something he'd never seen before. A sign. It hadn't been visible from his spot *in* the basket, but sitting there on the ground, he'd had a perfect view of its two words.

FOR SALE.

The first time Marcel had ever seen a sign like that was at the pet shop. He hadn't really understood what it meant then, but the day that Darla Pickens rang Ed's—Ed-who-liked-Marcel's-spines-until-he-didn't's—doorbell, holding a piece of paper with Marcel's picture on it and those same two words, he'd understood clearly.

"For sale" means that the pleasure of your company has a price. And in his experience, it really wasn't worth a lot.

Whether that sign was for Marcel's basket, or whether it was meant for him, it seemed pretty clear Dorothy wasn't planning on any more bike rides together.

As he and the bird had walked away from the backpack, the bicycle, the tree, the bird had looked back, shaking her head. "It's a shame," she'd said. "It was a nice nest. They usually are. But once you leave the nest, you can never go back. That's the rule."

Later, the *basset hound* had said something along those lines too.

What's done is done. The past is the past. All there is, is now.

And now, as he sat next to Tuffy, both of them staring at the morsel of Fruit Gem in the raccoon's hands, Marcel knew he had a job to do. Right now. In this moment.

Scamp was a clump of insecurities.

Old Ingot was a solitary tin can of tribulations.

Tuffy—the scared little guy just wanted to get home.

It had been only a couple of days, but Marcel found he'd grown to love this ragtag bunch. And he'd help them—love them—the only way he knew how.

A kind gesture, forgiveness—maybe not popcorn, but something equally good.

Something warm and wonderful.

"Tuffy," said Marcel, feeling his chest fill like a soda bubble and a small smile creep to his lips. "I'd like to tell you a story. It's a story about . . . a lion."

CHAPTER 16

The Growl of a Lion

MARCEL TOLD TUFFY THE STORY. ABOUT A few travelers (and a Toto). About the king of a forest, an animal with sharp teeth and terrible claws, an animal bigger and stronger than all the rest, an animal . . .

Who was scared.

"A lion," Marcel told him.

"A lion?" whispered Tuffy.

"A lion," Marcel said. "A cowardly one."

He told Tuffy about a journey, about a witch, about *fear*.

"You can't let fear chase you and gobble you

up. You gotta find whatever bravery is inside you, whatever strength you can find. Take courage from your friends. Courage, Tuffy! It only takes a little."

As Marcel spun the tale, Tuffy's eyes grew wider and his face grew brighter, for here, too, was his story.

"And last?" Marcel told him. "You look that fear in the face—and you growl."

"Like a lion," Tuffy whispered again, looking down at his mushroom medal and smiling.

"Like a lion."

Together, they crawled out from under the tree, ready to gather their friends, ready to meet whatever challenges lay ahead (even if they were still a little scared). The journey was waiting.

But first there would be apologies.

✦ ✦ ✦

Scamp stood there, shuffling her feet, her eyes rimmed red and raw.

Ingot cleared his throat. "I'm sorry for what I said. You should know I haven't thought badly of you or thought you were foolish. Truthfully, not at all. I don't think you're stupid. I—I actually think you're brave." He cleared his throat.

"I *am* brave," Scamp said, blowing her nose in her cape.

It took Ingot a while before he went on. "You are." He looked over at Marcel, Toto, and Tuffy. "Bravest of the bunch. Leaving home to help a stranger. Calling me out of my hidey-hole and shaming me into stepping out. Helping to take on Tuffy here and saving us all from the seagulls. You *are* brave. None of that makes you stupid." He gingerly took a knee to look straight into the eyes of the mouse. He sighed. "It makes you special."

Oh, Scamp. *Scarlet.* The Scarecrow to their motley crew and fastest sling-shooter in the forest. She was so many things.

She was fearless and full of ideas. She reminded Marcel of Dorothy. His Dorothy.

The fiercest of friends would.

A lump grew in Marcel's throat.

Ingot put out a hand. "Forgive me. Again." He grunted. "I've been alone a long time. It's no excuse, but everything, well, it all gets a bit rusty."

Scamp turned a toe in the dirt. She looked up at Ingot's outstretched hand. A shy smile tugged at her lips. "I forgive you, you old sour face."

"Well, it's not the first time I've been called that," said Ingot.

Scamp ignored Ingot's hand and threw her tiny arms around the squirrel's neck. "You looked like you needed this," she explained. "I'm sorry too."

"Er, thanks," said Ingot, looking a bit surprised, a little flustered. He patted her on the back until she let go, and Marcel wondered how long it had been since the squirrel had something so simple and necessary as a hug.

Ingot cleared his throat. "Well, what now? It's getting late. And we're still lost."

Scamp kicked at a few dry leaves at her feet. "I have no idea."

"How about a snack?" Marcel suggested, handing out blackberries.

They munched in silence, passing around the few acorns they had left and sharing the mushrooms and walnut Tuffy had found. Tuffy's stomach rumbled.

"Still hungry, Tuffy?" asked Marcel, looking over at his leaf-sack. He was hesitant to share the last of the Gems. He was using them for something else. Something important. Something for Ingot and Scamp.

Tuffy nodded. "Tuffy is missing his eat-boxes. Tuffy helps his mom and pop—he's smaller and climbs into all the eat-box crack-ers finding food." He frowned. "I am good at finding."

Marcel could picture it. Tuffy cracking open garbage cans and climbing into dumpsters to collect what few browning potato peels, slices of moldy cheese, stale doughnuts—preferably jelly filled—and the unwanted onions off someone's submarine sandwich he could find. People did throw away a lot of food.

Marcel's stomach rumbled now too as he thought about how much food was left in the theater after every showing. Nearly full boxes of peppermints, handfuls of yogurt raisins. Cinnamon

Snaps, Chocolate Buttons, and bucket after bucket after bucket of . . .

Popcorn?

Marcel sniffed at the air. Was it his imagination? He thought he caught a whiff of something.

"Do you smell that?" he asked. "That's not a woodsy smell."

Ingot and Scamp sniffed. Tuffy raised his nose and took in a whiff. "Tuffy's smelling something tasty."

Scamp's eyes grew wide.

"*Whizzlepop!*" she shouted. "We're back on the scent!"

At the mention, the entire forest seemed to open up, the spaces between the trees stretching wide, and the scent of popcorn tumbled in on every wind. It beckoned.

The four animals looked to one another. Marcel gave Toto a little hug.

"It's getting dark, but I think we should risk it," said Ingot. "We don't want to lose that smell."

Marcel agreed. “Would you like to lead us this time?” Ingot asked Scamp.

“No, thank you,” she said politely.

“But I thought you preferred it.”

“Not really. I just don’t like people telling me what to do.”

Ingot made a little noise and bit back a retort. “Good to know.”

Scamp thought for a minute. “Are you sure we should head out just now? I mean, I trust you and everything, but what about Wickedwing? She could be anywhere.” She noticed her cape was twisted and sat on a mushroom to fix it. “You really can’t be too careful with her, Ingot.”

Ingot’s eyes bulged. Just a little. “But you said . . .” He diplomatically chose not to finish his sentence. Marcel stifled a giggle.

Tuffy tugged at Marcel’s hand then, but Marcel had just noticed a strap on Toto’s pouch had come loose, and he set about fixing it. Tuffy tugged again.

Ingot couldn’t help himself, and he addressed

the contradictory Scamp. "I thought you said Wickedwing must've left for better hunting ground."

Scamp looked up from her cape. "I was *speculating,"* she answered. "It's getting dark. We should probably make camp for the night."

Tuffy tugged a third time, and Marcel looked up to find Tuffy, eyes wide as quarters, staring off into a shadowy thicket of gnarled grapevine.

Two enormous yellow eyes stared out from the thicket.

"I think," Marcel said, as softly as he could as he watched those two eyes narrow. He gulped.

"I think it might be too late."

CHAPTER 17

To Sidestep a Snatcher

INGOT QUIETLY STEPPED IN FRONT OF THE OTHER three without taking his gaze off the eyes burning into them. "On the count of four, you will run. Toward the popcorn scent if you can. Don't stop. If she gets too close, I'll lead her away. You just run. Run and don't look back."

"The count of four?" whispered Scamp. "Not like three?"

"One for each of us," Ingot said slowly.

"But you forgot Toto. He's five," Scamp whispered back.

"One."

Marcel, Tuffy, and Scamp each took a step into the popcorny breeze. The eyes narrowed again. The thicket crackled.

"Two."

Scamp's voice was trembling now. "Are we gonna make it?"

"There's no other outcome in my mind," Ingot said firmly.

The vines cracked. The eyes didn't blink, didn't falter.

Ingot gritted his teeth and braced himself. "Ready?"

Marcel wasn't sure they were. Ingot didn't wait for an answer.

"Three, four—go!"

As though they'd been shot from a cannon, they fled toward the popcorn smell. Behind them, a barrage of splintering vines cracked the air. The sound was terrifying.

But not as terrifying as the owl's cry. *"SCREEEE!"*

"Faster!" Ingot shouted.

They bobbed and weaved through the trees,

the bramble. The clouds parted and a little light opened up in the distance.

"To the light, to the light!" Ingot called from behind them.

Tuffy ran in front of Marcel, at Scamp's heels, and the pounding of their feet was a terrible drumbeat. "Don't stop!" Scamp yelled back to the raccoon.

Whoosh.

Inches above his head, Marcel caught a glimpse of feathers, feet, and flashing claws.

Wickedwing flew right over them.

"Keep going!" shouted Ingot. "She'll circle back!"

"What's she doing?" panted Scamp.

"She's playing with us!" said Ingot.

They scrambled over an enormous rock, and Tuffy lost his footing. Marcel heard him yelp as he tumbled away out of sight.

"Keep going!" Ingot shouted. "I'll get the raccoon. Keep for the sunset! Keep going until—don't even stop when you think you must! *Leap!*"

Marcel ran after Scamp, a cry caught in his throat.

Fear drummed into every inch of him. He took one look over his shoulder to see Ingot's tail disappear off the rock.

Ahead, Scamp was shouting. "It's opening up! I see light on the horizon! The forest is ending!"

"What then?" Marcel called to her. The trees thinned out. The light was growing.

"Ingot said go—even when—" Scamp raced beyond the last tree and came to an abrupt halt.

Marcel caught up, and his heart sank.

They stood on the edge of a high, windy precipice. Beneath them burned a field of crimson grass.

The sun slipped away and disappeared. In the distance, the lights on a cluster of tall greenish towers blinked on.

"The city," whispered Scamp.

Marcel looked down. "The fall."

They quickly turned to face the forest.

At the edge of the woods, a shadowy pair of giant wings folded in on themselves on the branch of an old tree. She was covered in darkness; all they could see were the lights of her eyes.

Click. Click.

The sound of her beak stole what was left of Marcel's courage.

Scamp whispered to Marcel out the corner of her mouth, "Where are they? Where's Ingot and Tuffy?"

"I—I don't know," answered Marcel. He tried to see past the trees.

Nothing moved. Just a few stubborn leaves twisting in the wind.

"What's she doing?" Scamp asked quietly.

Marcel swallowed hard. "Waiting."

The wind snapped at their backs. Scamp slowly raised her sling-shooter.

"I'm—I'm not sure you should do that," cautioned Marcel.

"Why?"

"This wind—what if you miss?"

Scamp gulped. "I miss and we're owl pellets." She lowered her sling.

Suddenly, from inside the forest, a volley of

pebbles clattered against the base of the owl's tree. Wickedwing looked down just as Ingot and Tuffy came barreling out. "Go! Go!" yelled Ingot.

"Go *where*?" screeched Scamp. "We're trapped!"

Before she knew it, Ingot flew past, holding Tuffy's paw and yanking hers as he went by. Tuffy grabbed Marcel's.

And the four went sailing over the edge.

They did not die as fast as Marcel would've expected.

"Spread eagle, spread eagle!" shouted Ingot. He and Tuffy had leaves clasped at their necks and around their middles, making something of a parachute, and Marcel was surprised to see both Scamp's and his packs doing almost the same. Scamp's cape whipped behind her. The wind screamed in their ears.

"The wind," hollered Ingot. "It'll hold you if you trust it! Arms and legs out!"

Marcel looked over at Tuffy. His eyes were as wide as lollipops and his mouth was open in a silent scream.

Scamp hollered. "What about Wickedwing?"

"Don't worry about her!" Ingot shouted into the wind. "Nothing we can do! Focus on what you can do something about!"

Unfortunately, the only other thing to focus on was the ground.

And it began to get very close.

"Everyone!" shouted Ingot. "Lean to the right! We're gonna aim for that bush!"

Four bodies tilted, and they sailed toward the giant prickly pillow of an evergreen bush.

"Straighten! Straighten! Tuck and roll when you hit!"

The bush grew bigger, wider. They braced for impact, and before they knew it . . .

They were welcomed into its waiting arms.

Which was an awfully nice way of putting it.

"Oof!"

"OUCH!"

"I think I swallowed a beetle!"

Marcel felt a branch snap, and he was deposited onto the ground in a heap. Luckily, he'd managed to land on his side. He checked to see if Toto was hurt and was relieved to see the cocoon wriggling with surprise but not pain, from what he could tell.

"Everyone okay?" Ingot tried to stand. His leg was bleeding, and he faltered over to where Tuffy was still clinging to a branch. Ingot's limp was much deeper now.

Scamp jumped from the bush, her walnut-shell shield dangling, her face full of scratches. She spat three pine needles into the dirt. "Where is she? Where's the owl?"

Ingot looked to the sky.

Wickedwing circled overhead and cried. She didn't appear to be making a descent, instead, the owl hovered near the top of the bluff.

Ingot breathed a sigh of relief. "Thought so. The cliff's the boundary. Though why she ever agreed to this whole boundary idea, I have no idea."

"Whose territory are we in now, do you think?" asked Marcel. He remembered the seagull's words. "The Whizzer's?" He gazed out at the field of little bluestem before them, red as embers in its fall color and the way the low sun touched every blade of grass and set it ablaze. He looked to the greenish hue of the towers in the distance.

The field of red poppies. The towers of the Emerald City. It was Oz at every turn.

"Whizzer?" replied Ingot. "Could be. Only option left."

Dark was creeping over the meadow, and Marcel suddenly felt too tired to wonder further. He noticed something was wrong with the remaining lens of his glasses and he took them off for a cleaning. Another crack.

"Come," said Ingot. "There's a knoll over there in the field. We'll get settled on the lee side. Out of the wind."

In less than an hour, Tuffy was curled up and asleep and Ingot had positioned himself next to a rock, wrapping long blades of grass around the wound on his leg.

Stars spiraled into the licorice-black sky, and

the puffs of their breath made small cotton-candy clouds against the night.

Marcel followed Scamp as she crawled to the top of the knoll and lay on her belly, chin resting on her paws. She stared at the green glow of the buildings springing up in the distance.

"I did it," she said as Marcel settled into the spot next to her. "I got you to your city."

Marcel's eyes drifted to Scamp's glowing city, and he felt a pang of sadness—for her, for him, for Tuffy.

They were not looking at his city. Not Shirley River.

The cluster of buildings and smoking stacks appeared to be a factory of sorts, and from the smell of it, it had something to do with popcorn. They hadn't been following the scent of the Emerald City Theater.

They'd been chasing a popcorn factory.

Could be they were farther from the city than ever.

Marcel felt the realization that he'd never get back to the hens and the theater sink in.

"I knew I could do it," Scamp said. "I knew I'd shoot straight." She rolled onto her back and looked up at the stars. "See that one?" She pointed to the brightest star. "See how it hangs there on the end of my sling-shooter? That's my special star. My papa gave it to me. That's how I know I'll always shoot straight."

Marcel recognized it. It was the North Star. The star that guides you home.

If only.

Scamp pointed to the bigger of the two sling-shooters in the sky. "The big one's my papa's. He taught me to shoot. Now he barely helps me aim." She sighed heavily and turned on her side to look at Marcel. "You like stars?"

Did he like stars?

Marcel imagined himself back in Dorothy's room, staring up at the fluorescent stars on the ceiling. *Pick one. Pick a star.*

There were oh so many stars.

If only every star had a wish and every wish came true.

Marcel had only ever wanted to be near her. And look at him now.

But when he felt Dorothy pulling away, there was only one thing to do, wasn't there?

"The past is the past. What's done is done. All there is, is now," the basset hound had said.

Marcel gave Scamp's special star one last look. And then he turned away.

Some things are too precious to hope for. And hope—he knew this well—can be disappointed.

"You like stars?" Scamp asked again.

For a long time, Marcel didn't answer. Instead, he began to hum. And then, with words he could only hear in his head, he found himself singing.

A song about wishing on stars.

A song about troubles melting away like candy.

Their song. His and Dorothy's.

But as the lyrics tumbled over themselves in

his mind, his thoughts snagged on two words.

He stopped humming.

"What was that?" asked Scamp. "It was kinda nice. Sad too."

She waited a minute or two for him to answer, but when he didn't, the mouse gave up. "Fine. Don't tell me." She stood to leave. "Good night, bristle-butt," Scamp said as she walked away, her tail dragging in the grass behind her.

He could still hear it. The tune he and his Dorothy sang to each other as Dorothy Gale crooned from the television.

Their "Over the Rainbow" song.

Marcel fell asleep that night to that one line, those two words, playing over and over in his head and dreamed of Dorothy.

Dreamed of baths in the kitchen sink where Dorothy never forgot to add his favorite rose-scented bubble bath and a rubber duck . . .

Karaoke under the twinkle lights in her bedroom with Marcel as the judge. He always awarded Dorothy first place. . . .

The high-tops Dorothy sewed for him, made out of red felt to match hers . . .

The Halloween she dressed up as a movie star and made a cardboard limousine to fit around her with a little driver's seat just for Marcel. He wore a bow tie. . . .

Gingersnap trails and giant bowls of popcorn.

The two words that warbled on repeat in the background were:

Find me, find me, find me. . . .

Wake up, Marcel. Wake up.

Marcel felt something cold kiss his cheek.

He turned over and buried his face under a leaf.

Marcel, wake up.

A gust of wind picked up the corner of his leaf and carried it away. Marcel's eyes were heavy, and his body was stiff and bruised from the day before. Somewhere between sleep and waking, he pinched his eyes shut tighter, hoping for a few more minutes of rest.

The whispery fingertips of snowflakes brushed against his face, his fur, his spines.

Get up, Marcel!

Marcel cracked open an eye.

Had he heard Oona's voice just now, or was it part of the dream?

A wintery wonderland broke out before him, fat snowflakes settling on the red and brown field all around. They covered Ingot and Tuffy in a thin white blanket.

Marcel sat up and blinked. He settled his glasses on his nose. "Oona?"

She was nowhere to be found.

But his eyes fixed on something else.

Something impossibly else.

A swarm of seagulls flew silently overhead.

Scamp was being carried off beneath them.

CHAPTER 18

Ozymandius Pott's Popcorn Emporium

IN SECONDS, MARCEL HAD TOTO STRAPPED TO HIS chest, and he, Ingot, and Tuffy were racing across the snowy field in pursuit of the gulls and the mouse-napped Scamp.

"Did you hear anything? Did they say where they were taking her?" Ingot shouted to Marcel. But Marcel had shared all that he knew, which was nothing. Ahead, the tall jade stacks of the factory chuffed white clouds into the sky.

Silos, great steel cylinders, squat with peaked tops, silvery and gleaming, stood like a row of soldiers beneath the smokestacks. As they grew close, a maze of steel ladders, bridges, pipes, and spouts connecting silo to silo came into view.

"They're landing! Over there!" Marcel shouted.

Like a settling fog, the seagulls descended, giving the three animals just enough time to cross the frozen fields. Just as the last bird touched the ground, the travelers reached the farthermost building. The hedgehog, the squirrel, and the raccoon crouched in the shadows.

The head seagull tapped his beak against a round hatch the size of a dinner plate a few inches off the ground.

An air shaft, Marcel thought to himself. *Or perhaps a popcorn hatch*?

The door opened with a screech, and to Marcel's surprise, the long nose of a rat popped out.

"What is it?" the rat squawked.

"Today's quota," answered the gull.

The rat looked Scamp over with a sneer. "It's a bit small, don't you think?"

"There was never a stipulation about size." Monk narrowed his eyes at the rat, who waited a moment to see if there was anything more the bird might offer.

"Fine!" said the rat. "Give 'er here."

Marcel, Ingot, and Tuffy watched as the seagull dangling Scamp by her belt moved toward the door. They could see the little mouse struggling to get free, a kernel of corn stuffed in her mouth to silence her.

"Come on, come on," ordered the rat. "Whizzer'll throw me in the popper if I don't get 'er up to the bridge soon."

"*Whizzer!*" whispered Ingot.

"Payment first," said Monk. "Push the button."

The rat sneered at the gull. His mouth curled back to reveal two long yellow teeth. "I hates doing business with *birds*."

Poking his nose out farther, the rat jabbed two fingers in his mouth and made a sharp, biting whistle. "Patsy! Nicky! Open the spout!" he shouted to two rats standing on a sort of large metal box beneath the silos.

"Aye-aye, boss!" they answered, and immediately they began to argue.

"It's my turn to press the button," said one to the other.

"You always press it, Nicky. It's your turn to press 'Off,'" the other argued back.

"I like 'On.'"

"You press 'Off!'"

"JUST PRESS THE BUTTON!" screeched the rat from the hatch.

Everyone watched as at the exact same moment, the two rats hit a large green button on the metal box.

With the sound of a freight train, an avalanche of corn kernels poured from a hinged spout on the metal pipes above and piled onto the ground below. The flock of gulls flapped to the edges and began to eat greedily.

Not a minute later, "Turn 'er off! Turn 'er off," the rat in the hatch called out.

At the press of a second button, the cascade of corn became a trickle, and the seagull carrying Scamp passed her through the round door and out of sight.

A growl rumbled up from deep inside Ingot's throat.

"No!" Marcel yelled, but the wind caught it and swept it away.

Tuffy threw his paws over his eyes and whimpered.

"Nice doing business with yeh," said the rat. He slammed the door.

The last kernel was snapped up, and the gulls began to fly off.

Ingot turned to face Marcel and Tuffy. "Follow me. Say nothing. Look as tough as you can . . ." His gaze fell on Tuffy, and Ingot made a little sigh. The raccoon still had his paws over his eyes. Ingot reached up and mussed the raccoon's fur into an angry mess, pulled Tuffy's paws from his face, and waited for the raccoon to open his eyes. "Just cross your arms, Tuffy. Cross your arms and look mean. You need to do this for Scamp, you hear? I'll take care of the rest."

He led them out of the shadows of the great smoking stacks and over to the round door.

Ingot rapped very hard on the metal. It echoed somewhere inside.

Once more, the door opened, and the rat's nose popped out. He looked very surprised to see a grizzled squirrel, a glowering hedgehog, and a grim-looking raccoon on his doorstep. "What is this?" he demanded.

Ingot's voice was firm. "We're here to see Whizzer."

"No one sees Whizzer unless Whizzer wants to see them. Read the sign." He pointed to an ornate sign tacked to the side of the building before popping his nose back inside and clanging the door shut.

Marcel adjusted his glasses and read aloud the looping letters:

OZYMANDIUS POTT'S
POPCORN EMPORIUM,
SUPPLIER OF ALL YOUR POPCORN NEEDS
(SPECIALIZING IN CARNIVAL AND MOVIE-THEATER SALES)

NO TRESPASSERS ALLOWED.

Ingot rapped on the door again, harder this time.

The door opened once more. "WHAT?" squeaked the rat.

"I am Ingot Graytail, governor of the southern forest!" shouted Ingot.

Marcel gasped. He couldn't help it. Ingot sounded so princely. Marcel stood straighter.

Tuffy, concentrating hard on looking tough, barely registered a reaction.

Ingot's shoulders were firm, and his voice shook with anger. "You will take us to see Whizzer, or I can assure you, you *will* lose your tail, sir!"

The rat blinked at them, unmoved. "If I fell for that every time, I woulda lost more than my tail a long time ago." He looked the three of them over. "Whizzer meets with fiends and friends, and neither apply. Good day!"

"Wait!"

Marcel had not expected to speak. He'd planned not to, in fact.

And yet here he found himself with three pairs of eyes waiting to see what he'd say next.

"I . . . I . . ." He was a jumble of thoughts. He

only knew he had one chance to get past the door. One shot to save his friend.

There could be no messing this up.

The gatekeeper.

The thought popped into his head. The gatekeeper for the Emerald City—he remembered it now. But how had Dorothy and the Scarecrow, the Tin Man and the Cowardly Lion gotten past?

It was the mention of the ruby slippers.

His Fruit Gems!

Marcel tore the sack off his back and pulled out the last candies from inside. "Here! Look here! We have these! And . . ." His mind was racing. "And we know where to get more! We want to make an . . . an *agreement*!" He stole the seagull's words.

The rat's eyes grew wide.

Marcel held up the candies a short distance from the rat's long, pointy nose.

The rat sniffed at the limes with unrestrained interest. "I . . . uh . . . yes. Waits here." He slammed the hatch closed.

The three travelers waited anxiously.

But their worries were soon allayed. The door swung wide and the rat bade them enter. "Come in, come in! You should've said you were looking to deal! Whizzer is pleased to meet with hawkers of all kinds."

They followed the rat through the hole and the tunnel beyond. "This way! This way!" urged the rat.

They passed single file out of the tunnel and into the factory, climbing four stories of metal piping and crossing grated bridges with a million holes you could see through to the bottom. The factory was quiet now, but at the foreman's whistle the vats would be bubbling, machinery chugging. Soon what seemed like all the corn in the world would fly through sorting machines, pop in great circular ovens, and be boxed and bagged along every imaginable sort of slide.

They climbed higher still.

At last, high above it all and far away from peeping eyes, in an area of the factory left to gather dust, they passed down a hallway. Around a corner and just beyond a forest of retired file cabinets left littering the hall, they reached a wooden door. Beside the door there was a loose slat in the wall. The rat knocked three times.

"Enter!" called a deep voice from behind the wall.

The rat pushed the wooden slat aside and stepped back. "Go ahead," he said. "Whizzer will see you now."

"This isn't a trick, is it?" growled Ingot.

"Now, what good would there be in that?" the rat said. "What do we need three extra mouths for?"

Marcel, still holding his Fruit Gems, swallowed, but Ingot nodded to him, and the hedgehog stepped inside.

It appeared, Marcel thought, to be a room frozen in time, a room where long-ago tools and machines came to die. Everywhere you looked, on the sloped shelves, the wooden tables, and strewn about the floor, there were rusty old parts, nuts and bolts in varying sizes, wrenches thick with grease. Dust floated through the air, and the smell was all turpentine, wood, motor oil, and of course, popcorn.

A mischief of rats guarded the room on every side. Sneering, sniggering rats.

"Welcome" came a slick voice at the far end. "So, you've come to ol' Whizzer to make a deal. Let's see what you've got."

Marcel, Ingot, and Tuffy followed the voice to where a pile of old machinery sat stacked into a sort of throne.

The fattest rat Marcel had ever seen sat atop the great chair, his enormous belly lopping over his knees. He looked to have been fashioned almost without legs, only feet. *Tiny* feet.

"I am Whizzer. The great and powerful," boomed the rat.

"And I'm Ingot. The old and unimpressed," Ingot said under his breath.

"And who might we have here?"

Introductions were made. "Well, well," said Whizzer to Ingot. "I've heard of you, squirrel. You disappeared from the southern forest, let's see . . . years ago, wasn't it? Everyone guessed you were dead. It is a surprise, you coming here to grovel to me."

Ingot stepped forward. "We're just here to make a trade," he said. "You have something we want, and we've got something you want." He grabbed the candy from Marcel's hands. "These! We've got an unending supply, and we've heard how fond you are of trades."

Whizzer eased off his seat and stood. Marcel tried not to gawk. The rat looked impossibly rounder now. Like a furry watermelon with a tail. Whizzer held out his hands.

Ingot placed the lime candies in each of the rat's paws.

Whizzer bent his head to give them a deep and thorough sniff. "Very nice, very nice," he said. "And you say you have more?"

"Tons more. Boxes and boxes more," answered Ingot. He shifted his feet, and Marcel noticed the ragged grass bandage on Ingot's leg was blood-stained. Hopefully, Whizzer hadn't noticed.

The enormous rat narrowed his eyes and considered Ingot's words.

"Hmm," he said after a minute. "You said there was something you wanted from me." He tossed the two Gems onto the throne behind him. "What is it?"

"Your prisoner!" Ingot said sharply. "We'll trade you the secret of our stash for your prisoner."

The rat smiled wide, and a poisonous look crossed his face. "My prisoner—and what would you know about that?"

"She was one of our party," Ingot said quickly. "She was taken by the seagulls and we followed them here. Hand her over and we'll tell you where to find your candy. Take the deal. One prisoner for a lifetime of sweets." Marcel felt Tuffy grab his hand and quickly let go.

(The raccoon must have remembered he needed to look menacing.)

The rat smiled again and regarded his visitors. "I will take your offer. Follow me."

The travelers traded worried glances as they fell into step with the rats.

Whizzer led them out a broken window, and then they were outside, high above the factory. Below, the grass was white with snow. A grid of metal ramps and bridges led to eight enormous silver silos hunkering in a row. They crossed the slippery metalwork single file and passed the towering silos one by one.

The wind threatened to toss them over the edge, but they braced themselves against it. With each gust, metal pipes screeched and strained against their moorings. A bolt broke loose, and they watched as the seagull's corn spout began to swing as if pushed by an invisible hand.

At last they reached the final silo. The bridges ended in a small deck where there huddled another group of rats, smaller in size but no less mean-looking. Whizzer led them through the whiskery mass of tails and teeth.

The rats parted to reveal Scamp on the other side, tied to a railing overlooking a forty-foot drop.

"Here we are," said Whizzer. He waved his arm with flourish. "Your prisoner."

The pack of rats giggled and cheered.

"Untie her," growled Ingot.

Whizzer lowered his hand. The rats went silent. An evil grin was pinned to Whizzer's face. "Now, why would I do a thing like that?"

Suddenly, vermin on every side took hold of Marcel, Ingot, and Tuffy. Sharp claws bit into their fur as Ingot and Marcel struggled to get free. Tuffy, looking woozy, squeezed his eyes shut.

"We made a deal!" shouted Ingot.

"Did we?" said Whizzer, feigning innocence. "I don't recall."

"Let us go!" the squirrel ordered.

The huge rat laughed. The bulge of his belly wobbled.

The rats began to tie them to the railing next to Scamp.

"Ah, my friends, I'm afraid it's much too late for that," said Whizzer. He pointed a claw toward the sky, where a small winged dot was taking shape in the blowing snow. He grinned. "From here on out, you can take it up with her."

The dot grew bigger, the wings, wider.

"My God," said Ingot, when the thing came into view.

Ingot said nothing more; there wasn't need. For this, Marcel knew, could be only one thing, the witch they'd managed to elude for so long.

Here, now, was Wickedwing.

CHAPTER 19

The Largest Smallest Rescue

AS THE GREAT OWL SPIRALED DOWN, WHIZZER explained the details of the agreement. It seemed to please him.

"The forest, the farmhouse, the factory—those are the boundaries. After the mice poisoned the old settlement yonder, the witch began to hunt here. Picked off a bunch of our own before I ventured a deal." He leaned close. "See now, the owl had herself too many of those chipmunks and rabbits who'd sipped that poison water. *They* were all well and fine after—a few sips never hurt anybody, and word of poison water gets out fast. But the owl . . ."

Whizzer sat back, looking very proud. "She can't sniff it out. She's got eyes, but her sniffer . . ." He tapped his nose and grinned. "There's poison running through her blood. Real and actual poison. One more bite could kill her. So, we bring her a nice poison-free meal every day and she agrees to leave our kind alone. No hunting on factory grounds—that's the deal."

"What happens when she gets a hankering for rat again?" Ingot growled.

"Oh." Whizzer stepped close to Ingot. "I don't think she will. Half of us got rat poison running through our veins too. We rats can build a tolerance. Nicky and Patsy there were basically raised on the stuff."

Everyone looked over to the two rats from earlier, who were pushing each other a little too close to the edge and giggling like fools.

Whizzer walked over to Scamp. The little mouse's eyes were wide as she remained tied to the railing. The rat wiggled the kernel of corn, making sure it was wedged tight in her mouth. He leaned in and seemed to muse to himself. "I wouldn't put it past the old girl to nip us just for spite, but one little offering and she leaves us alone. You know, it's never too hard to find a lone straggler snooping around in hopes of snatching a kernel or two—but look!" He whirled around to face the others. "Today we've brought four!"

The rats on every side cheered. Marcel shuddered. Ingot looked fierce and ready for a fight. Only Tuffy was undisturbed. The poor thing had fainted dead away.

They hadn't even bothered to tie him up.

Whizzer went on. "Once the seagulls heard about our little agreement, they wanted in on the deal. Offered to supply us a few tasty tidbits a week if we let them partake of our corn. Less work for us."

So that was it. The gulls had carried off Scamp as a trade. Marcel felt his insides set to a rolling boil for possibly the first time in his entire hedgehog life.

Whizzer drew closer to Scamp and sniffed.

"Seems like we got ourselves a tainted mouse here. Guess we won't be offering the owl four after all. This one will be *our* little snack."

Above them, the mighty owl-witch began to descend, and the sea of rats flattened out, a shivering wave of rat fur with tails tucked beneath them.

Only four figures stood above the crowd: Whizzer, Ingot, Marcel, and Scamp. Tuffy lay like a lump on the metal grating.

The owl's wings were eerily silent. Not a whisper, not a *shush*. There was only the trembling of a hundred rats and a warning on the wind.

Clank. Clank.

The sound of the owl's talons made Marcel's knees go weak as she landed on a pipe not far away.

Whizzer straightened himself and sucked in his belly. "Your Highness!" he shouted. "I daresay we've brought you here a smorgasbord of delights this morning! Take your pick; don't be shy! Take one, take all—it's entirely up to you." He leaned closer. "But if you *do* take more than one, consider it a deposit. We've got a few days' worth of credit right here."

The owl's eyes bored into him, and she clicked her beak once. Sharply.

"Of course, if you're needing a bit extra . . ." Whizzer's eyes danced from the owl to the bridge to the far-away door to the factory, a trace of nervousness in his voice. It seemed the rat was searching for a place to escape—if he happened to need it.

Marcel's heart raced. They were tied up, trapped. There was no way out. The only possible escape, Marcel noted, was the forty-foot drop to the frozen ground below.

"Which would you like first?" asked Whizzer. "I've got a fat little raccoon right here, or how about this squirrel?" He stepped over to Ingot. "Meat's a bit tough, I'll bet. There's a well-fed hedgehog there. Just need to get around all the sharp parts first."

The rat went over to where Scamp stood tied to the iron bars. He grinned. His long yellow teeth gleamed. He made a special point of winking at

Ingot as he offered up Scamp next. "How about this little appetizer?"

The owl clicked her beak again and flew from the far railing to a spot closer to where the three animals stood pinned to the rail. One much, *much* too close for comfort. She took a step toward Scamp.

"Ah!" said Whizzer. "I see you've made your choice. And an excellent one at that!"

Whizzer leaned over to Ingot. "Doubt there's enough poison in that mouthful to hurt her much. I guess we'll see!" he squealed.

Ingot strained against his bindings. "Get away from her!" he shouted to the owl.

Marcel wiggled wildly, trying to loosen his fastenings.

Tuffy remained blissfully unaware in his current state of unconsciousness. Marcel envied him.

Wickedwing took a step closer. She was massive, and so near, Marcel could smell the sweet scent of blood on her breath.

"Won't take more than a second," Whizzer

called over to Ingot and Marcel. He smiled at the witch, who was now just inches from Scamp. "She likes 'em in one bite."

Zing.

Something shot past the owl's head, missing her by mere inches.

Zing, zing, zing, zing, zing, zing, zing!

Corn kernels and pebbles flew in every direction. Whizzer ducked. The owl's head swiveled about, trying to spy whatever it was that was interrupting her meal.

The missiles kept coming. *Zing! Thwing! Thwack! Ping!* They began to hit their targets. First a rat. Then another. Soon, rats on every side were springing up and holding heads, sides, arms, and noses.

"I'm hit!"

"Oh, I'm bleeding!"

Marcel, Ingot, and Scamp could only try to get as small as they could manage, tied up and in the direct line of fire like they were. Tuffy, poor Tuffy, lay in his heap, unaware.

Zing! Thwack! Ping! Smack! POP! The last sound had an air of finality about it, and the owl-witch rose up, flapping frantically and screeching.

And suddenly everything went very silent except for the owl's pained, exquisite cries.

Marcel squeezed his eyes shut. He was either about to be lunch, or about to be shot, and neither possibility afforded him any comfort. He felt Toto wriggle against his chest and the sharp edge of the wind as it sliced a cold blade between each and every one of his quills. He counted the seconds.

One . . . two . . . three . . .

A familiar voice bellowed from somewhere below them. "Whizzer of Ozymandius Pott's Popcorn Emporium, unhand them!"

Marcel's eyes popped open. The owl was flapping high above. Straining to see through the one broken lens of his glasses, Marcel scanned the ground, and there below, standing firm in the whipping wind . . .

Was the whole tribe of Mousekinland.

Mice men, women, and mouselings. Every one of them wielding a sling-shooter trained on the owl, Whizzer, and his lackeys.

The rats of the Emporium were scuttling down to a lower bridge, which ended in a metal staircase that zigzagged toward the ground. They froze near the middle of the pass at the sound of the mouse mayor's voice.

Mayor Mortodellus Mousekin, stepping away from the rest of the townsmice, addressed the rat leader. "Unhand them, Whizzer, or prepare to meet your fate!"

Scamp at last managed to spit out the corn kernel that had gagged her. "Papa!" she screamed.

"Scarlet!" The mayor ran forward, trying to lay eyes on his daughter. The rest of Mousekinland stretched their sling-shooters farther and perfected their aim. "Scarlet, where are you?"

"I'm here, Papa!" Scamp yelled. "I'm all right!"

The mayor's eyes circled back to Whizzer. "Do it," he ordered. "Do it now!"

The rat king sneered and bared his teeth. "It's

a hungry day at the Emporium that I listen to the likes of *you*!"

While the mouse and rat leaders traded barbs, up on deck, Tuffy stirred.

"Tuffy!" Marcel whispered. "Tuffy, wake up!"

The young raccoon stirred again, and his eyes blinked open. He rubbed them and sat up.

"Tuffy," Marcel said before the raccoon had time to faint away again. "We need your help. You need to chew through this string here. You need to help get us free!"

The raccoon's eyes were the size of Chocolate Buttons, but he nodded and did what he was told.

Mayor Mousekin was still thundering from below. "You'll be held accountable for your crimes—you and every one of your associates! How *dare* you take the witch's side!"

"I've *taken* her side because that's the side that benefits me! Don't pretend you wouldn't do the same if you were in my fur." Whizzer began to walk the lower bridge again. His tail curled, and he took leisurely strides toward the stairwell.

Nothing about him or the rats that followed appeared bothered in the least.

Tuffy finished gnawing at Scamp's bindings, and as soon as Scamp was loose, she whipped her sling-shooter from her pack, grabbed the single kernel of corn that had been wedged into her mouth, and flew to the edge of the railing.

"I've chosen my side," Whizzer was saying. "And you'd do well to do likewise. You will leave Oz's Emporium one way or another. I suggest you do it alive!"

"However we leave, it won't be as traitors!" Mayor Mousekin bellowed back.

The rats were now bunched together in the middle of the lower bridge. Marcel spotted the corn pipe dangling directly above them.

Next to him, Scamp was taking careful aim. She slowed her breathing. She steadied her shaking paws. The blowing snow swirled about her, but she was fixed on one thing, one single thing alone.

The green button.

"You're outnumbered!" Whizzer shouted into the wind. "The owl will be sick of mouse flesh by the time she's done with you!"

Scamp narrowed her eyes, made a final adjustment, and waited for a second's break in the wind. When it came, there was no hesitation.

She let the kernel fly.

Zing!

Pink!

It was such a small sound. Barely louder than the cry of a kitten.

But what came next was a roar.

Rat chins and noses rose at the sound as tens and hundreds and thousands of pounds of corn rained from the spout over their heads. The force of the corn ripped the bridge from its bolts. The metal, bent and crushed, teetered before letting go. Corn continued to pour, stopping only when the silo went dry.

When the last kernels fell, like drops in an ocean, there stood a twenty-foot mountain of corn.

Not a rat remained.

Scattered and sore, the broken lot of them were chasing after their king.

As away above the treetops flew a Whizzer and a witch.

CHAPTER 20

The Mouse's Goodbye

THE MICE OF MOUSEKINLAND AND THE TRAVelers welcomed one another with open arms. But not before Scamp was reunited with her father.

"Papa!" she yelled, running into the mayor's arms.

"Scarlet. Oh, my Scarlet."

Scamp buried her face in his fur. "How did you find me?" she asked, as the rest of Mousekinland, now up in the warm and dusty storeroom above the factory, brought in a feast of corn and set to work building carts and bins and beds for the little ones.

The mayor's eyes were wet as he looked at his

daughter. "We followed your trail, of course," he said, to Scamp's surprise. "It must have been shortly after you left—you and the hedgehog. We were ransacked by crows. The milk snake, as you know, may have hunted us, but we found out she kept prowlers away too. We were defenseless against the crows. They took everything, everything." The mayor blew his nose on a tiny leaf handkerchief. "I thought you'd been taken by them." He covered his face, and his whole body trembled. "It was the darkest moment of my life."

"I'm sorry, Papa. I'm so sorry," Scamp said, wiping away tears.

Mice all around began to pull nuts, bolts, washers, and wood chips up to a long, thin board they'd fashioned into a traditional Mousekin table. The largest of them was pounding thumbtacks into the floorboards, which made pretty good stools to sit at. The mayor nodded at him.

"Barley Fitchsnout sniffed you out. Found your trail. Pieces of those weird fruits you left behind on the road and beyond. When he came back with the news, the whole town was in agreement. Every one of us would come looking for you."

Scamp took a seat on an old iron cog next to Marcel and frowned as a few mouselings chased one another around a box stuffed with tools. "But what trail?" she said. "I didn't leave a trail."

"I did," said Marcel, breaking off a small piece of the lime candy he'd been offering the mouselings. "I left a Fruit Gem trail. For you to get back. Just in case."

Scamp narrowed her eyes at him. "That was highly dangerous, Spike. I thought I told you to throw those away."

"You did. But being lost is dangerous too," Marcel said quietly.

Scamp turned back to her father. "But why would you risk it? Why follow me? I led you all into danger. The one thing we hide from!"

"Scarlet," said Mayor Mousekin. He pulled over a spool of wire and sat. "You're part of us. Without any one of us, we're no longer Mousekinland. You were missing, and there was only one thing to do.

There's not a rock we would've left unturned to find you."

"But I ran away—I mean, I had some pretty good reasons, and the hedgehog needed me. But I still ran away from home! Through cornfields and marshes and woods—I don't even remember half the places we went to!" Scamp was scratching ferociously at that old spot on her cheek. As the truth dawned on her, her hand froze mid-scratch. "I really never would've found my way back," she whispered.

She looked straight at Marcel, and her eyes grew misty again. She looked down at the floor and said a shy, "Thanks."

"You left home, so home leaves everything to come find you. It's the Mousekin way," said the mayor. "Trails are good too."

Something broke in Scamp then. She threw back her head and began to wail. Truth be told, it was not a pretty sight. She was loud, and red, and snotty. "But everyone hates me!" she cried. "Everyone thinks I'm foolhardy! I don't *think*;

I just *do*. Stupid me—I'm the reason we left the farmhouse in the first place. Plus, I burned down the field! And the bridge! Now we're homeless again because of me!"

Mayor Mousekin looked up at the ceiling and shook his head. "So much fuss and fire. Listen." He pulled his daughter close. "You were wrong to leave. You were rash, and you are right—you didn't think. But you are not stupid."

He tapped her forehead. "This head is filled with ideas. Stupidity is going into battle not thinking there's an enemy. Stupid is putting your feet to the fire and not expecting to get burned. I can't say I'm happy about it, but you knew the risks and you took them anyway. And you did it for the noblest reason of them all—you did it for a friend."

Mayor Mousekin looked over at Marcel and then back to Scamp. "I spoke with the squirrel. And, well . . ." The mayor looked a little sheepish. "He helped me see some things. Wisdom is more than facts. I see that now. To face your fears, to put your faith in something bigger, to be willing to sacrifice for another—these are the least stupid things of all. I'm sorry I made it out to be different."

Scamp was hiccuping now. Every sixth hiccup was punctuated by a burp.

From behind a stack of wooden crates, a tiny mouse with big ears crept over to Scamp with a large kernel of corn in his hands. Four more faces peeked out from behind the crates. The mouse blinked at Scamp and held out the kernel.

Sniffling, Scamp took it, and the little mouse skipped back to the group of mouselings. "She touched my hand! She touched my hand! I'm never gonna wash it ever again!"

"What's the difference? You never washed it anyway!" said his friend.

"We love you, Scarlet. Me the most," said Mayor Mousekin. "I know I haven't said yes to a lot of things. I thought I was protecting you. I didn't want to see you hurt. I wanted a whole *life* for you. I'm not sure I wasn't stealing some of it in the process. I should've given you some freedom, let you practice dreaming a bit. To *live* is a risk. I told myself that by hovering over you I could control you, control everything." He shook his head. "I think I held on too hard."

Scamp stopped sniffling, and she seemed to be considering all that her father had to say. As she did, her face began to brighten. There was a smile on her lips by the time she answered. "Does this mean I can get a sword?"

The mayor threw up his hands in dismay. "What will I do with you, girl?" he cried, but he was laughing as he grabbed her hand and turned to survey the brand-new bustling mouse town in the old workshop high above the factory. "Just look at it," he said proudly. "Look what you've done."

Before them, little houses were being built out of pipe fittings, wicker baskets, an old leather boot. Newly fashioned carts, made of faded screw boxes and rusty bolts, toted corn. A hundred sling-shooters hung in a line.

With the rats gone, Mousekinland was being remade. Here.

The mayor's face became serious. "Scarlet. You have a choice to make, now. You'll have to choose whether or not to go on with your friends or stay. As you've come so far, I know now that I cannot make that choice for you; I cannot make you stay. Does the journey continue, or have you come to the end? Where does the next road lead, and where is your place now? Away? Or here with all this . . . ?" He extended his hand.

The table was spread. A hundred seats on either side filled with mice. Old Mrs. Sniffers danced on her chair. Barley Fitchsnout balanced precariously on the edge of his thumbtack seat before the needle broke and not just he, but the mice on either side of him tumbled to the ground.

A kernel at each place, and at every place a smile, a laugh, a word of thanks.

Just then, a group of young mouselings rounded the corner at a run, pulling Tuffy and Ingot behind them. A huge smile was plastered to the raccoon's face. He was wearing a moth-eaten glove for a hat.

Ingot was another story. The mouselings had dressed him in a skirt made of a crinkly piece of foil they'd found. His cheeks had been colored with a bit of red paint, and the bristly top of a paint-brush was broken off and placed bristles-down on his head. "Never should've left the tractor," Ingot grumbled.

"Attention everyone! Attention!"

A trio of fiddlers, tuning their instruments, silenced their strings. Voices hushed.

The mayor of Mousekinland climbed atop a box and looked down upon the rows of mice seated at the table. Marcel, Tuffy, and Ingot sat too.

"We have much to celebrate today!" announced the mayor. "Lost things have been found. Those searching have made homes. We have new friends with us, and food. Let us partake of this feast with thankful hearts. To Mousekinland!"

"To Mousekinland!" all replied.

The band struck up; the meal was shared.

Merrymakers laughed and joked and told tales of their adventures into the night. Mothers and fathers tucked mouselings into bed. Even the dust motes seemed happy to take a turn on the dance floor.

When quiet came and the only light was a slice of moonlight on the floorboards, the four friends (plus a cocoon) found one another on a windowsill overlooking the snow-covered fields and forest beyond.

Tuffy smiled sleepily. Marcel fiddled with his glasses, taking them on and off, trying to buff away the scratches on his one remaining lens. Ingot remained silent.

Scamp was scratching. At her cheek, behind her ear, the back of her knee, and everyplace in between.

"Good heavens, put something on that, would you?" grumbled Ingot.

Scamp clawed at her cheek. "I can't put anything on it! It's a botheration breakout!"

Marcel crawled around Ingot to sit next to the overwrought mouse. Tuffy grabbed one of Scamp's paws and watched the snow drift into the fields. After a minute, Marcel felt a tiny mouse hand slip into his.

"What will you do?" Marcel whispered.

"She knows what she needs to do. That's why she's scratching," said Ingot.

Tuffy's eyes were sleepy, but he looked at Scamp tenderly. "You're staying here, huh, Scamp?"

The little mouse blinked, her mouth slightly open. "I . . . I . . ."

"You are," said Ingot. "We know it. You know it. It's the end of the line."

Marcel squeezed Scamp's hand gently. "It's okay, you know. You belong here. With your father. Mousekinland wouldn't be the same without you."

Scamp tore her hand away. "I can't leave you, prickle-head! You need me! How are you gonna get home without me? And you, too, Tuffy! Who's gonna look after you?" She turned her exasperated face to Ingot then. "Who's going to tell you you're entirely wrong about everything, you old, awful bristle-tail?"

"Ha! I'm not sure there's another living thing that could take your job," answered Ingot, but there was a smile curling the corners of his mouth. "You know what you need to do, mouse. You've had your journey. You've made your rescues. You've proved your merit and mettle. Maybe it's time to know what it's like to be at peace for a change. Life's more than just a battle."

Scamp sat there wiping her nose on her cape and taking it all in. She scratched again, but a little less and lesser still, until finally she looked up at the squirrel.

"I can still get a sword, right?"

Ingot laughed heartily. "I fear for whoever—or whatever—tries to stop you."

That night, the four travelers—the hedgehog, the mouse, the old gray squirrel, and the raccoon—sat at the windowsill long into the night. Not sleeping. Not talking. Letting the hours stretch as wide and long and slow as hours do.

Because when morning brings a goodbye . . .

Every second with a friend isn't nearly enough.

CHAPTER 21

Stowaways

AT THE FOREMAN'S WHISTLE, THE RUMBLE OF motors and the chugging of factory machines began.

"You can't go by foot, that's certain."

"The owl's got a bone to pick. She'll get you before you make it to the trees."

"I'd stick to what's safe if I were you. Don't leave."

Scamp and her father, Marcel, Ingot, and a few of the Mousekinland elders were sitting in a circle, trading ideas about the next leg of the journey. Tuffy, having gotten bored with the conversation after only a minute, blew hot air onto a far window and was having quite a fine time drawing . . . well, it wasn't apparent exactly *what* he was drawing.

"Wings is what you need. Not sure how you get there otherwise," said a tall mouse.

"How do you feel about waiting till spring?" asked a short one. "I got a cousin that makes a river trip to the city every spring. Carved a boat out of a gourd. Not sure that'd be big enough, though . . ."

They were getting nowhere, and no one was as frustrated as Ingot, Marcel, and Scamp.

"We aren't making any progress here," said Ingot. "We don't have wings, and nobody's building any boats. There hasn't been one reasonable suggestion yet. Anybody else got any bright ideas?"

There was murmuring among them, but they sat the next few minutes in silence.

Tuffy had his nose pressed against the window. "There's honkers out there," Marcel heard him say to himself. "Lots of honkers."

"What's he talking about?" yelled a very old, hard-of-hearing mouse.

"Honkers!" the mouse next to him yelled back.

Marcel remembered Tuffy talking about honkers when they first met him. Something about honkers squashing things up. He'd left the city in one. *What were they again?*

"Wait a second," Marcel said to the group. He crawled up the workbench and pulled himself onto the sill.

Behind the factory, on a sea of black pavement, parked a long line of trucks. They butted up against a loading dock in different shapes and sizes, some more like box trucks, others hauling freight cars. Their sides blazoned with advertisements like SLAPPY SAL'S DELIVERY LINES, THRIFT MART, FARNSWOLD FREIGHT AND SHIPPING.

"That's it!" cried Marcel. "You've figured it out, Tuffy!" He pointed out the window and looked to the group. "We hitch a ride. That's how we get back to Shirley River."

The rest of them crowded around.

"How d'you know they aren't mouse-trapped?" questioned the tall mouse.

"Ludicrous! No way you'll make it!" protested another.

"My cousin hitched a ride on a truck once. Wound up in a city. Met his wife there and came back with ninety-six kids," said the short mouse. "What a lady."

Ingot sounded cross. "What makes you think it'll work? What in tarnation do those trucks have to do with your theater?"

Marcel pushed up his glasses and grinned. "Popcorn."

Marcel told them about the Emerald City Theater's concession stand. He'd never actually seen a delivery truck, mind you, but he'd heard them. Every Thursday before the weekend rush, a truck, coughing and spluttering, pulled up to the green-tiled entrance and dropped several plain, cardboard boxes filled with sacks of corn for the popping. Marcel had rummaged through those boxes in the past, hunting for stray kernels. If they could just get on the right truck, maybe, just maybe, he'd be delivered right to the theater's front doors.

"Well," said the mayor. "It's the best idea we've heard yet."

"Humans don't take kindly to hitchhikers," said Ingot. "Especially those with fur."

"My cousin hitched a ride on a truck once," said the short mouse, peering down at the trucks and nibbling at a patchy spot of fur. "Humans don't fret over what they don't see."

"And neither do I!" said the mayor.

Scamp shot a tiny finger in the air. "*That's* not true!" She quickly slipped it back down when her father gave her a stern look. "I mean that's not *always* true . . . sir."

The mayor softened. "Yes. Well. You've got a point. But I do think if we can keep them out of sight, they've at least got some chance." He scratched his chin. "I think we can find a way."

Ingot let out an exasperated sigh. "You still haven't answered the most important question." He pointed out the window. "*Which* truck?"

Ten pairs of eyes stared through the glass at a line of several dozen trucks.

"It's a Thursday," whispered Marcel, spotting a blinking sign below them. "Thursday, December 3rd, 9:02 a.m. It has to be down there."

Everyone looked to the mayor. He nodded.

"Then, we begin."

It took Mousekinland all of twenty minutes to have a lightweight crate cobbled out of an assortment of pine boards, complete with air holes and a crudely fashioned shipping label that read:

SHIPING ADRES:
THE EMERALD CITY MOVIE THEATER, SHERLY RIVER

RETERN ADRES:
OZYMANDIUS POTT'S POPCORN EMPORIUM

(VERY IMPORTINT.) FRAJIL.

"It's perfect," said Scamp.

"It's a shot in the dark," grumbled Ingot.

Scamp looked over at Marcel and smiled. "It's your ticket home."

Whatever it was, it was certain to be a terrible hassle to get down four stories to the dock.

"Not so!" shouted Scamp. "See, I came up with this invention. I call it . . . a pulley."

A group of mouse scouts were sent to spy out possible points of entry. Another group set about fashioning Scamp's pulley system out of rope and a large, empty cable reel. The bravest were chosen for the last leg of the journey: getting the crate to the right spot on the dock and nailing the travelers in. Scamp was the first chosen.

While the mayor and elders finalized plans, Marcel, Ingot, Tuffy, and Scamp stood huddled together, trying to think up words to say. Tuffy sat in a lump looking very sad. Scamp was snuffling, snotty, and bleary-eyed.

"You sure you don't need me? I mean, I could go with you and try to get back. How will you ever make it without me?"

"We'll be fine," said Ingot. "I made it into old age without your assistance. I'm pretty sure I can get by."

Marcel smiled weakly at Scamp. "What Ingot means is he'll miss you. Very much."

Scamp shoved packages wrapped in paper and string into their paws and looked away. "These are for you."

They thanked her and opened them in turn. Tuffy's gift was Scamp's cape, now boasting an extra-long string to tie around his neck. He hurriedly slipped it over his head. The cape was far too small, but it gave him a very noble look.

"Wearing a cape makes you look braver, even if you don't feel it," Scamp said to him.

Ingot's gift was Scamp's walnut-shell shield. "Your head and your heart. Those are the two most important places to protect," Scamp said.

Next it was Marcel's turn. Inside the paper lay Scamp's old sling-shooter.

"I got more," Scamp said briskly. "You'll need to keep watch and fight anything that comes after you. You won't have me to help you, but you can borrow my special star. Shoot straight. And don't miss."

Gifts and food for the journey were packed into Mousekinland leaf sacks. When it was time to leave, Scamp wailed as she clung to Tuffy and Marcel in the largest of mouse hugs. When it was Ingot's turn, she looked up at him, frowning, and said, "I'm not gonna miss you at all, you bushy old geezer." But she clung to him the longest, and never once did Ingot try to let go.

"Trucks are being loaded," interrupted the mayor. "It's time to go."

It took every one of the travelers and a group of twenty Mousekins to lower the crate over one of the metal bridges to the open floor of the factory, and a group of the bravest volunteers to position it. They hugged the walls as they pushed it toward the loading doors. Every time a bootstep was heard or a voice was near, the group scattered to hide behind boxes, bins, and machinery.

At length, a voice crackled over a speaker.

"Attention! Attention! There will be a brief meeting for all employees and drivers in the Pott's Cafeter-ium. Remember your clipboards; shipping lists will be handed out. Thank you and have a poptastic day."

"Jackpot!" whispered one of the mice.

Footsteps shuffled by. Voices grew fainter. A door clanged shut.

"Now!" shouted the mayor.

Every mouse assigned to the crate flew into position.

Marcel, Ingot, Tuffy, and Scamp ran down the dock, passing trucks with their backs open and piled ceiling high with boxes, searching for the one that might bring the travelers home.

Truck after truck didn't feel right to Marcel. He ruled out the largest of them straightaway. He checked license plates. Not California. Not Missouri. Definitely not Alaska. He read the peeling words on the sides of the remaining trucks.

HOG APPLE FARMS: PORK PRODUCER. And in small letters *(We'll haul your slop. Our pigs eat anything.)* No.

PIXIE'S CARNIVAL SUPPLY: OUR COTTON CANDY, CORNDOGS, AND CARAMEL POPCORN ARE MAGIC! Nope.

CEREAL SOURCE: GRAINS ARE US. Doubtful.

They were coming to the final truck, a small white box truck.

"End of the line, kid," said Ingot.

Marcel closed his eyes and prayed this truck would be the one.

There was no big sign on the box of the truck; there was nothing at all. But stuck to the driver's door was a small green logo with a picture. Marcel saw the picture before he could read the words.

It was a hot air balloon.

The words formed and became readable. FLYING BALLOON FREIGHT, it said simply. Marcel stopped.

It was a sign. This was the flying balloon the Wizard of Oz had assured Dorothy could get her back to Kansas—back home. This was their truck. He knew it in his heart.

He was as sure as he'd ever been of anything.

"This is it," he told them as the mice trailed behind, pushing and pulling the crate. "This one goes to the theater."

"You're certain?" asked Ingot.

"Without a doubt," answered Marcel.

The whistle blew overhead.

"Hurry," shouted the mayor as they pushed the

crate to the edge of the dock. “Get inside!”

Tuffy, Ingot, and Marcel, with Toto strapped to his chest, climbed into the box, just as the door on the other side of the factory squealed open and footsteps and voices shuffled in. There was no time for lingering goodbyes.

The mice hefted the wooden top onto the crate and nailed the travelers in. Scamp whispered through the cracks in the wood, “Either you’re gonna find home or home’s gonna find you. Either way, you’re gonna get there. I know it.”

Through a small hole, Marcel saw the shadow of her tiny paw resting against the wood as the last nail went in. “I love you,” she whispered.

And then she was gone.

CHAPTER 22

The Emerald City

BOOTS CLUMPED PAST, AND A DOOR CREAKED open.

"Come on, Terry! Get moving! We're already behind."

Another set of boots came running. "Coming! Had to stop to tie my boot!"

"Is that the driver?" Marcel whispered to Ingot, who was peering out one of the holes.

"He's getting in," Ingot answered.

The sound of the rolling door on the back of the truck made the travelers jump. Tuffy clutched the string of his cape and squeezed his eyes shut.

"Make sure you lock it this time!" they heard the driver call. "We almost lost a few boxes on the last run."

"They're leaving, Ingot!" Marcel's stomach flip-flopped. He felt sick.

The other man finished setting the lock. "I got it. I got it. Start 'er up!"

The truck roared to life, and Ingot frowned darkly. "Nothing we can do."

"Scamp!" Marcel shouted through the cracks of the crate. If there was anything that could be done, she was just the mouse to do it.

Just then, they heard a *zing*.

"Yeeeeow!"

Marcel looked to Ingot. Ingot looked to Tuffy. Tuffy opened his eyes and squeezed them shut again. They held their breath, Scamp and her trusty sling-shooter on every one of their minds.

Their hearts, too.

"Something bit me!" shouted the man at the back of the truck.

"Aw, quit your bellyaching, Terry. There's no bugs in the middle of winter."

"No really! Something bit me! I'm not kid—" Something clattered off the side of the crate. "Hey, what's that?"

They listened as the man read off the shipping label. "This is weird," he called over to the driver. "I never seen any label looking like this. Looks like some kid wrote it."

"They probably couldn't fit it in one of the big boxes. Just hurry up and throw it in."

Ingot, Marcel, and Tuffy let out a collective sigh of relief as they felt the crate being lifted and heard the lock open and the door slide up. "Weirdest box I've ever seen," the man muttered to himself. He pitched the crate inside.

The travelers went tumbling over and under and around each other. Ingot and Tuffy tried hard not to complain about Marcel's spines. And again Marcel found himself trying to protect Toto. Just like at the beginning.

The door slammed shut and the truck jerked to life.

Before they knew it, they were hurtling down the road at top speed.

Marcel looked to the others. "I wasn't sure we could pull it off."

"It remains to be seen," said Ingot.

"Tuffy's going home," said the little raccoon, his eyes bright in the small blazing lights of the back of the truck.

Ingot grimaced, but he nodded. "Yes, kid. You're going home."

The ride was bumpy, the smell of exhaust was thick in the crate, and turning corners was a particular trial. (Someone always ended up with a spine in their side.)

But Marcel felt a flutter in his chest.

Soon.

Soon he'd be back under his warm popcorn bucket with the hens on each side. He wondered where he'd find them. Waiting in the air shaft? Back in the balcony? Had they hidden behind the stage or in some forgotten corner? Wherever he found them, there was one thing he knew: They'd celebrate the end of this long, harrowing ordeal with a trip to the slush machine.

Ah, the slush machine. Marcel wouldn't normally be so intrepid. He'd always been content to scrounge the floors and topple into wastebaskets for every meal. And though he'd taken his fair share from the soda dispensers, they were constantly leaking anyway. It seemed a far cry from thievery.

Somehow the slush machine felt different, though—special. He'd choose the Passionfruit Punch flavor. He couldn't help but think his return would be something like a romantic celebration.

Scratch that. He wanted the Blaster-Berry.

Once, just once, he'd fill an extra-large cup to the top with that beautiful blue slush. It would be a celebration indeed. If only it were a Saturday.

He would have loved to arrive just in time for the twelve o'clock matinee.

The truck began to make stops, the drivers calling them out as they went. *The Picture Palace.*

Morty's Movie Madness. Little by little the back of the truck began to empty as theater after theater received box after box after box of popcorn kernels.

At one point, Tuffy snoozed. He was clutching Scamp's cape, sucking his thumb, and dreaming about something adventurous Marcel guessed from the constant movement of his legs.

Marcel moved over to Ingot. As he did, he noticed the old squirrel's leg was still bleeding under a fresh bandage. The wound had looked angry before, but now it was positively frightful. "Ingot?"

Ingot sat against the side of the crate, his eyes closed. "What is it, hedgehog?"

Marcel looked at the bandage. "After we get to Shirley River—to the theater, I mean—what will you do next? Will you try to get home?"

"That's for me to worry about," said Ingot.

"Well," said Marcel, "I guess I just wanted you to know that if you wanted to stay at the theater with me and the hens, you'd be welcome. For however long you'd like to stay. Even forever."

Ingot's eyes remained closed. "I'll keep it in mind."

The day wore on. *The Films de France Theatre. Hal's Hollywood Heaven.*

When it seemed like they would travel in the back of the Flying Balloon delivery truck for the rest of time, they came to a halt and heard one of the men say, "This is it. Emerald City Theater."

"We're here!" Marcel cried. "We made it!" Tuffy rubbed his sleepy eyes, and Ingot braced himself in a corner, waiting for the box to be pitched out.

"This can't be it," they heard the driver scoff. "You must've read the address wrong."

"I didn't, Morris! I swear I didn't. Look, it says right here on the list. 204 Peachtree Street."

Morris grumbled. "You sure that's a four and not a nine?"

"Yep."

"And there's no stop on the order? Nothing like that?"

"Nope. Think they made a mistake?"

Marcel was confused. How on earth could you

miss it? The gleaming ticket booth. The enormous marquee. You don't see so obvious and beautiful a theater every day. And why on earth would Gomer Dupree stop ordering popcorn? What was a theater without popcorn?

"I don't know why they gotta switch up our routes every week. How's it my problem somebody got it wrong?" the driver blustered.

"Well, it says right here—three boxes to 204. This is the place."

Morris smacked the steering wheel. "If this is it, this is it! Just leave it there. Not our problem!"

The door to the cab opened. "Whatever you say, boss!"

"Well, that didn't sound promising," said Ingot as the men walked to the back of the truck and opened the rolling door.

Cold air rushed into the cracks and holes of the crate. A few boxes were slid out and dropped on what Marcel guessed was the sidewalk.

"Don't leave it there," corrected Morris. "Put it over . . . Just put it over there."

The travelers listened as the boxes were transported a little distance away.

"Don't forget this extra one," said Terry, and he pulled the wooden crate from the back of the truck.

"Yeesh. You weren't kidding. Strangest delivery box I've ever seen."

The crate was bouncing, and it was difficult to catch sight of anything through the small cracks. The crate *thunk*ed on top of a box, and the world went still.

"That's it!" called Terry.

"On to the next!"

The back door clanged shut. The cab doors opened and closed. The engine started up with a crack, and soon the truck was chugging down the street.

"I can't see anything. You see anything?" Marcel tried to get a look outside, but the boxes were blocking him.

"I got a good view of a hubcap," said Ingot. "And a gum wrapper."

Tuffy took a big sniff. "Tuffy's smelling home!"

he said excitedly. "Tuffy's smelling eat-boxes!"

Marcel took in the nailed-in walls of the crate and his eyebrows furrowed. "I guess we didn't think about how we'd get out of here."

"Bunch of geniuses," growled the old squirrel. He thought a minute. "Only option is breaking out. If we all run for one side, maybe we can topple it. It's worth a try anyway."

Ingot, Tuffy, and Marcel (with Toto) stepped to one side. On the count of three they rushed to the opposite side, throwing shoulders, sides, and hips into the box.

It moved a hair.

"Again!" shouted Ingot.

They repeated this again and again, each time moving the crate little by little.

Ingot's leg began to bleed through his bandage. "Again!" he shouted. "Again, again!"

They slammed their weight into the crate one final time. It teetered on the edge of the box and pitched. Box, squirrel, hedgehog, raccoon, and cocoon went tumbling over.

The crate crashed onto the street and split open. The travelers flopped out into the slush. Marcel grabbed his glasses from the slop of the wet snow and scrambled to his feet. He threw his spectacles on his nose and rushed around the boxes to lay eyes on his and the hens' home at last.

Only he couldn't see anything. Snow covered his lens.

He rubbed his glasses against his fur. The snow smeared, but it was better. He threw them back on his face, ready to gaze upon the great and gleaming Emerald City Theater.

It was not there.

CHAPTER 23

A Billion Pinpricks of Light

THE EMERALD CITY THEATER LAY IN A PILE OF brick and plaster, broken beams, and smashed tile. Glass glinted from the rubble like diamonds. The velvet seats, a great heap of crimson, looked like half-melted Cinnamon Snaps lumped together. The great movie screen lay torn in two, and the pointed ends of broken pipes and cracked lumber pierced it in a thousand places.

"Well, that explains it," said Ingot.

"Auntie Hen! Uncle Henrietta!" Marcel cried. "Are you there? Can you hear me?"

Only the wind answered, howling and swirling the snow. Traffic hooted and hollered behind them. Buses and delivery trucks coughed by.

"We're gonna need to find cover before someone spots us and sends the raccoon right back," said Ingot.

Marcel heard him but was fixed to the sidewalk.

Ingot stepped in front of him. "Marcel, they aren't here. They probably got out. Either way, we're in a dangerous spot." Ingot's eyes were soft. "We're going to have to find a place to hole up. Need to get off the street. You think there's somewhere safe in there we can get to, out of the cold?"

Marcel stared off at the ruins of his theater. From under the screen, the heavy velvet stage curtain peeked out. Marcel pointed to it. "It'll be warm there," he said dully.

They picked through the bricks and glass carefully. And what a sight they must seem, Marcel thought bitterly. A bone-tired hedgehog with a broken pair of spectacles and a tiny cocoon. The raccoon, with his miniature cape and his hair in fourteen different directions, jumping at every dark corner and needing a good dose of coaxing from Ingot.

The squirrel. Ingot wore Scamp's shield like a helmet as he picked through the debris. His bandage was filthy and wet. His limp was worse than ever.

They found a bit of tunnel under the rubble and followed it. It ended in a pocket of space where the movie screen tented up above them and the velvet curtain rolled beneath their feet. Ingot collapsed into the thick fabric and closed his eyes.

Tuffy crawled over to a bright-green something and picked it up in his hands. He licked it. "I am liking this mess-hole! It's delicious!"

"What have you got there, Tuffy?" Marcel asked. He took the raccoon's hand and opened his fingers.

Inside Tuffy's palm lay a lime Fruit Gem. Marcel closed the raccoon's fingers around his prize. "Keep it." He remembered then what Uncle Henrietta always said about the lime ones. "They taste like grass."

Ingot spoke up. "We'll get some rest now. Head out when it's dark. Tuffy's parents won't venture out till later anyway. We'll have a look then."

The hours from afternoon until dark, however, were long and lonely. While Ingot slept, Tuffy scavenged every Fruit Gem, yogurt raisin, and Chocolate Button he could find scattered in the dust and glass. He managed to collect four Gems (all lime), twelve Chocolate Buttons, one yogurt raisin, two Coco-nutties, a caramel, and five Toffee Beans, pushing them into a pile and staring at them adoringly.

A despairing Marcel watched Tuffy as he ran back and forth in search of goodies, commenting only when he chose anything that wasn't, in fact, food. The raccoon kept getting mixed up with the pieces of emerald-green tile, thinking something so colorful must surely taste good. (It didn't.)

Toto, as ever, just wriggled.

Marcel felt lost. Here he'd dragged his friends to the city, to what he thought would be a home for one, if not all of them, if need be. But his plans, just like the theater, lay in ruins. He would never again breathe in the scent of hot buttered popcorn or curl up in the balcony under his jumbo bucket. He'd never again scrounge a candy supper for himself and the hen sisters. An extra-large-size Blaster-Berry slush all his own was the thing of dreams now, and the giant screen had showed its last film. There'd be no more seven p.m. showings. No *War of the Wombats*. No *Robots Take Mars*. No *Love on the Louisiana Turnpike*.

He'd never again watch his beloved *Wizard of Oz*.

And without a theater, without Oz, why should Dorothy come to visit? His Dorothy.

But that was silly. He'd given up the dream of her coming to the theater a long time ago.

He worried now about Auntie Hen and Uncle Henrietta. Had they escaped? Were they able to get out before all this? And if they did, where had they gone?

Auntie Hen had always been a little soft and Uncle Henrietta just a little too hard to make it on the streets, Marcel thought. Two red hens living—where? In a rat-infested alley? On a windy fire escape with a pot of begonias? Marcel imagined them hunting for scraps on the street. A Chinese noodle here, soggy bits of cereal thrown from fifty different strollers there, fighting the pigeons for a crust of bread.

Marcel shuddered. What had become of his hens?

And what would become of him?

Was it like Ingot said? Had sheer bad luck done this? Would the same luck have him back on the streets again?

It seemed there wasn't a doubt.

Why, oh why, was the world such a dark place?

Marcel thought of losing Dorothy. He thought of Ingot and how very alone the squirrel was in the world. He thought of Tuffy, separated from his parents. And now Scamp was gone. Marcel was happy she'd found her place again in Mousekinland, but he felt the loss of her to their little group too.

Marcel considered all this as he crept to the edge of the curtain and peered out at the stars igniting above him.

The night sky peered back.

Marcel fixed his gaze through his one acceptable lens, and he noticed something. It was this:

That even in the darkness, there are a billion pinpricks of light.

He shook his head. That sounded a little too hopeful, in his experience.

Marcel crept back under their makeshift tent.

Wrapped in the curtain and shivering a little, Ingot stirred. "It quiet enough out there yet?" he asked.

"Almost," said Marcel.

Tuffy straightened his cape and pulled his candy stash closer. "Tuffy's ready."

When it was sufficiently dark and the noises on the street had quieted to a whimper, the three friends tramped out. They stayed close to buildings and under anything they could, and alley by alley, they searched the city's dumpsters—Tuffy's eat-boxes. Quite a few were lorded over by rats, and one particular alley they avoided altogether at the earsplitting yowling of a dozen cats.

Dumpster to dumpster they went, asking any friendly animal they passed if they'd seen any raccoons about, and did they know where the best eating was.

They'd been at it for hours when Ingot collapsed. "I need to rest a few minutes," he said in his scratchy growl. "My leg . . . It just needs a rest is all."

The others agreed, and they found a comfortable spot out of the wind, in a darkened bus stop with a good view.

The streets were dressed for the holidays. Giant tinsel snowflakes, lit by tiny glowing lights, hung from the lampposts. Christmas trees and menorahs brightened many a frosty window. Somewhere, carols played over a speaker, and the world should have felt wondrous had they not been hurt, and homeless, and lost.

They weren't far from the theater now, having

walked several blocks, then doubling back. In fact, from his spot in the bus stop vestibule, Marcel could see the hole it had left on the opposite side of the street farther down. The sight of it wrecked him.

From around a corner, an old-fashioned pickup truck rumbled up to the curb in front of the theater and sat idling. There was a particular sound to the truck that Marcel thought he recognized.

"You see that?" he asked, craning his neck for a better view.

"See what?" said Ingot.

"That truck there." Marcel squinted through the scratched lens of his spectacles. "What's it doing?"

"How should I know?" said Ingot. He groaned as he unwrapped his grass bandage. He found a strip of newspaper and began to rewrap the leg again, tighter.

The truck grumbled and waited.

"Something's . . . I—I need a better look," said Marcel, and Tuffy followed.

"I'll catch up in a minute!" Ingot called after them.

A long line of cars sat parked on the street, and Marcel and Tuffy dropped into the gutter.

The truck's headlights glowed a dull yellow, and a freshly cut pine tree with a sprinkling of snow poked out of the back at a slant. Exhaust puffed from the tailpipe and hung in the air like fog.

The cab was dark and nebulous, but as Marcel and Tuffy neared, Marcel thought he felt a hint of recognition at the driver's outline. They scuttled closer and hid behind the tire of a low sedan.

They were about to move another car forward when the pickup's door opened with a squawk. A foot planted itself in the snow, and then another. A man stepped out onto the sidewalk, hoisted the popcorn boxes into the back, and beheld the broken theater. He spoke.

"We had a good run, didn't we?"

It was Gomer Dupree. Night janitor, office manager, popcorn popper, and owner of the Emerald City Theater. He had on a wool hat over his bald brown head and a scarf around his neck.

He bent down and pushed a hand into the

debris and pulled something out, perhaps a shard of green tile, a scrap of velvet, or a piece of gold-painted wood—some memento to remember the theater by. He shoved it into the pocket of his coat. "We sure had a good run, old girl. Yes, we did."

He turned back to the truck and opened the door. "Come on, now, you two. Scoot over."

Marcel stepped closer.

"Let's go home, ladies!" said Gomer Dupree. He started to climb into the driver's seat but paused. "Darned light. Must be a short in it or something."

There was the sound of a few thumps as Gomer Dupree banged against the overhead light. It flickered and blinked on. Marcel never expected to see what he saw next.

There, on the dashboard of the pickup, sat two red hens.

"Auntie Hen! Uncle Henrietta!" he called out in barely a whisper.

Next to Marcel, Tuffy's eyes went wide. "Those are Marcel's hens?"

"That's them." Marcel choked on the words.

The janitor, satisfied, jumped into the driver's seat and slammed the door. Marcel heard the shift of gears, and the truck started forward.

"No!" Marcel shouted. But what could he do? He tore Scamp's old sling-shooter from his pack and fumbled trying to place a pebble in the pocket. Next to him, Tuffy's eyes narrowed.

"Watch out for the honkers—honkers squash you up," the raccoon mumbled to himself. He looked down at his mushroom medal. "But those are Marcel's hens. And Tuffy has his cape. . . ."

The truck was advancing. Closer, closer. It was nearly upon them when all at once a look of sheer determination crossed Tuffy's face.

Tuffy's cape fluttered out behind him with a heroic air as he bellowed, "Oh no, you're not taking those hens! Tuffy is being a—a—"

Tuffy bolted out into the street, and Marcel heard his cry as the truck barreled forward.

"Tuffy is being a LION!" he yelled, and he planted himself there in the middle of the street in the direct path of a honker.

CHAPTER 24

Surprises in the Night

THE TRUCK ROARED DOWN.

Marcel ran from his hiding place. "Tuffy, no!" he shouted.

Somewhere in the distance, Ingot was shouting too.

But Gomer Dupree's pickup didn't slow. In fact, it picked up speed.

Tuffy—there wasn't time to reach him.

The instant before the truck bore down, Marcel turned back to avoid the tread of the tires. He could hear Ingot yelling, the groan of the engine, the *slock* and *slush* of the snow.

And then the truck was beyond them.

Marcel stood, his back to the street, shaking. He could not look.

Ingot raced past him into the road, his face wild with fear. "What are you, *crazy*?" he cried.

He was not speaking to Marcel.

And only then did the hedgehog have the courage to turn.

There Tuffy stood, shining under the light of a streetlamp. He was frozen in the middle of the lane, one foot planted in front of the other, one arm thrust forward, palm out, as if signaling for the truck to stop. The miniature cape floated out behind him in a daredevil way.

A tiny daredevil way.

The squirrel had taken Tuffy by the shoulders and was shaking him. "It went right over you!" Ingot turned to Marcel. "It went right over him! I don't believe it!"

Marcel, still in shock, stared open-mouthed at the two of them, but his eyes flicked back to where the pickup chugged into the night.

The pine tree bumped along in the back, and he caught a last glance of the hen sisters' wide feathered ends, before the truck spun down a side street and disappeared.

Something deep inside told him he'd never lay eyes on his hens again. He'd certainly never help Auntie Hen out of her theater seat when it ate her up. He'd never need to save all his Toffee Beans for Uncle Henrietta. He'd never wake to the murmuring and soft clucks of two sleeping chickens and fall asleep to their arguing banter.

A sad smile lingered on his face even still.

Auntie Hen and Uncle Henrietta looked happy, Marcel thought to himself.

Somewhere on the next street, the pickup truck backfired, a loud bang rippling over the buildings, like it agreed.

Ingot was still shouting. "This raccoon's crazy! Absolutely nuts!" And then the tired old squirrel began to laugh. A great, roaring laugh. "That was dumb, kid. Really dumb. But brave, too." He patted the raccoon's cheek proudly, and Tuffy's resulting smile was as long and sweet as a Licorice Twist.

"Like the lion," Tuffy said. "Tuffy was wanting to be like the lion, even though he was scared. And like Scamp. Tuffy wants to be just like her—he wanted to save Marcel's friends. But . . ." His face fell then as he looked over to where Marcel stood at the side of the road. "The honker didn't stop."

Marcel smiled weakly. "That doesn't make you any less brave, Tuffy." He crept out into the street under the watchful light of the streetlamp. "You're not a cowardly lion—you're not even a brave one. You're a raccoon. A good, brave raccoon and a friend. Being brave isn't being something you're not. Courage is knowing everything you are, fears and all, and stepping out anyway." Marcel smiled wider now. "You didn't let your fear be stronger than your fight, Tuffy. You tried, and that means very much to me. Thank you."

"Sometimes living, breathing, getting up and facing the day is all the brave you need to be," Marcel heard Ingot say quietly.

Somewhere, a little way down the street, something chittered in the night. The three of them—the raccoon, the squirrel, and the hedgehog—froze in the dim glare of the streetlamp.

"Don't move," murmured Ingot.

In the darkness something stirred. Two shapes bumbled over the curb and into the street a few yards away. They crept into the light of the next streetlamp and sat on their haunches, their black eyes looking straight at the three travelers.

Gray fur. Fuzzy ears. Black noses and whiskers and dark masks around their eyes like a couple of bandits. Striped, bushy tails. Tiny hands wringing with worry.

Tuffy took a hesitant step forward. "Mama? Papa?"

"Tuffini?"

"Tuffy, is that you?" The voice cracked.

Tuffy began to trot, then run. The two raccoons did the same. "It's me!" Tuffy shouted. "It's your Tuffy!"

When they reached one another, Tuffy flung

himself into the furry arms of his parents, and there, in the frozen night, as the two older raccoons wept and laughed and peppered him with kisses, the cowardly-but-not-too-cowardly Tuffy's journey out of the woods came to an end.

Marcel and Ingot could only stand in amazement. First in shock, then with crazy grins on their faces. Ingot, though he tried to hide it, wiped away a few tears of his own.

When he'd finally calmed down enough for words, Tuffy spoke through broken hiccups. "How"—*hicc*—"how did you find me?" *Hiccup!*

His father looked down at him with glad eyes. "We were on the next street over, searching as we do—we've *done*—every night since you disappeared. We'd already made our way down this street and the one before, the one after, and were about to begin the next block when we heard shouting—"

"Shouting," cut in Tuffy's mother. "And then the loud bang of a honker. We've always been so worried you'd be squashed up."

"We had to make sure it wasn't you."

Tuffy squeezed the two tighter.

"Our eat-box is twenty blocks away," said Tuffy's mother, her eyebrows furrowed, but her voice was tender. She lifted the little raccoon's chin and searched his face. "How in the world did you get this far?"

A car turned down the street toward them, and Ingot cleared his throat. "I think you'll find he got a lot farther than that, but for now, we should find a safer place to chitchat. Over here." He beckoned them over with a wave of his hand, and the group of animals followed the limping squirrel to a nearby newsstand barely big enough for one person to stand inside. It was dark and shuttered, but Ingot reached up, took Scamp's walnut shell from his head, and rummaged around inside it.

"Learned a thing or two about being prepared from that mouse." He pulled out a metal pin he'd snatched from the factory workshop, climbed to the newsstand's counter, jammed it in the sliding door's lock, and jimmied it. The lock sprang open.

Together, they lifted the overhanging door and wedged a rock in the crack just big enough for them to squeeze inside.

With luck, Marcel found a flashlight, and he flicked it on. Everyone sucked in their breath.

On one side of the newsstand sat row upon row of newspapers and magazines, but on the other, floor to ceiling, was arranged every sort of candy you could dream of. It was like being in the theater again, only better. Chocolate Buttons, Cherry Dips, Marshmallow Kisses, Peppermint Sticks. Gumdrops, lemon drops, Licorice Twists, and Treacle Chews. There were toffees, taffies—every possible kind of sugary goo.

"Hm," said Ingot.

"Check the garbage," Marcel and Tuffy's parents said in unison.

Sure enough, there was plenty to go around. Tuffy selected a half-eaten box of taffy, and his parents each took Peppermint Sticks. Marcel chose three caramels and tore into them hungrily.

Marcel looked over at Ingot, who was hunched in a corner. "You're not eating?"

"Not hungry. Mind your business," the old squirrel snapped back.

Even though he knew Ingot was in pain and probably exhausted, Marcel winced.

With mouths stuffed with sweets, Marcel and Tuffy did their best to relay all of Tuffy's exploits to his parents, who here and there gave startled squeaks. When the story was over, both raccoons looked pale.

Tuffy's father swallowed painfully. "Well," he said. "That was quite the story. I—I don't know what to say. . . ."

"Oh, my baby!" wailed Tuffy's mother, clutching her young kit to her breast. "You could've been killed! You must have been so scared. And to think! We could have missed you! If we hadn't heard that shouting, that honker—I can't bear to think it. But still, after everything we taught you, why did you run out into the street?"

All eyes turned to the little raccoon.

Tuffy swallowed the mouthful of taffy he'd been gnawing on. He stood, Scamp's old cape hung limply down his back.

"Tuffy was scared," he said, looking down at his feet. "Scared of the honkers, scared of mean-trees and scream-birds and snatchers. Scared of Whizzer and his fat-rats. Scared of everything." Tuffy looked up, a blush rosying his cheeks. "Tuffy was scared . . . but he can be brave, too. Like Scamp, and Ingot, and Marcel. Tuffy was brave because he was seeing he *can* be brave. Brave like his friends." He looked at Ingot and Marcel. "Brave *for* his friends."

"Brave for his friends," repeated Ingot softly.

"We need to be getting back, I'm afraid," said Tuffy's father. "Got twenty blocks to cover before daylight." He turned to Marcel and Ingot. "Will you join us? You saved our boy. Our home is yours."

"And leave my peace and quiet? Never," growled Ingot. "Besides, that tyke is too much trouble for this old squirrel." It would have come off as coarse if he hadn't given Tuffy's chin an affectionate tap.

Marcel hadn't really thought about what was next. With no theater, no hens, and now no Tuffy to care for, he was free to do whatever he pleased.

But one look at Ingot shifting his injured leg and grimacing was all Marcel needed to make his decision. "I'm going to stay too," he said.

They filed out of the newsstand into the December night. A snowflake fluttered down and landed on Marcel's nose. Then another. The midnight sky became a ballet of white snowflakes—dancers twirling in lace-tipped skirts, falling to the ground all dizzy and spent.

Ingot was the last out, and Tuffy, who was the larger of the two, swept the old squirrel up in his arms. "Tuffy will miss you!" he said.

"Yeah, yeah. I'll miss you too."

Tuffy put Ingot down. "When will I be seeing you again?"

It was a perfectly fair question, but the look on Ingot's face when Tuffy asked it was one Marcel couldn't discern. They watched as Ingot turned to go back inside, coming out a moment later with the front page of the prior day's *Shirley River Herald*.

"Here," said Ingot, laying the page on the ground and swiping a half-melted chocolate from Tuffy's hand. He ran the chocolate over his hand and made a handprint on the newspaper. "There. You got that to remember me by." Ingot handed the chocolate to Marcel, who repeated the gesture.

When Marcel was finished, Tuffy grabbed the newspaper and clutched it to his chest. "This is my favorite thing. My favorite thing from my friends."

Marcel and Ingot watched them go. The raccoons stuck to the shadows when they could, and when they couldn't, Tuffy never failed to turn under the glow of the streetlights, waving heartily just one more time.

"Let's get to it, then," said Ingot, turning back in the direction of the theater. His footprints left behind a trace of blood in the snow.

"Ingot, you're bleeding," said Marcel.

"Everything bleeds," the squirrel replied. "Keep walking."

"But . . ."

Ingot turned to face him. "I'm bleeding, Marcel. Yes, I am. Been bleeding a while now. Will probably continue. But here I stand. We all bleed. We just keep walking."

It wasn't far. Just over a block. It shouldn't have taken long, but Ingot's injury now seemed too much for him. The squirrel dragged, though his brow was set as ever.

They were nearly to the wreck of the theater, when Marcel caught a bit of movement in the corner of his glasses. A reflection.

An eye, the flap of a wing—talons.

And then a sinking feeling.

"*Get down!*" shouted Marcel, pulling Ingot to the ground next to him just as the owl passed over, her claws missing them by the fringe of a feather.

Wickedwing screamed a furious scream and swooped out of sight.

"She'll be back!" Ingot yelled. "We need to hide!"

Marcel wrenched Ingot off the ground, braced an arm under the squirrel, and made for the pile of bricks. They ran. Ingot slipped in the snow and stumbled. Marcel pulled him to his feet. "We're nearly there! Just a few more feet!" Marcel urged.

The shriek of the owl pierced the air around them, and Ingot found fresh motivation to cover the last few feet at a run. They scrambled up the bricks and metal, looking for a big enough opening to squeeze through and hide.

"There! Over there!" Ingot shouted, spotting a black crevasse in the snow. They tripped toward it, fast as they could. Marcel felt a sharp piece of glass rip through his foot. Instinctively he stopped to grab hold of it as Ingot disappeared inside the opening.

"We're in!" Marcel heard Ingot shout . . .

Just as claws sank into his shoulders and his feet broke away from the ground.

CHAPTER 25

A Heart That Beats

TIME SEEMED TO SLOW. AS MARCEL'S TOES GRAZED the top of the rubble, what ran through his mind wasn't fear or whether or not the inside of an owl's stomach was as inhospitable as it seemed, it was . . .

Dorothy.

A cry escaped his mouth, and hot tears sprang to his eyes. He was flying. And then . . .

Two hands clamped around his ankles, tight as iron shackles.

"Not today, Witch!" Ingot cried.

Marcel felt the tug. One above, one below.

"I got you, Marcel!" Ingot shouted. "Don't worry. I got you!"

The snow swirled around them as Wickedwing tried to catch air. But the wind and the weight of the two animals tugged her back toward the ground, and soon Ingot's tail trailed over the rubble.

A metal pipe shot out of the wreckage like a bent flagpole on a mountaintop, and Ingot hooked his back feet around the pipe and held on. Marcel felt the owl's fiery talons sink deeper into his shoulders as she tried to wrench him free.

"I . . . won't . . . let . . . go," Ingot spat through gritted teeth.

Searing pain shot shoulder to ankle as every part of Marcel felt like it was being ripped in two. And then . . .

He was tumbling into the broken bowels of the theater, he and Ingot, rolling end over end, head over tail. Marcel crashed into a piece of the old mahogany balcony, managing once again to spare Toto. Ingot rolled farther, coming to a stop on a large chunk of the roof, spread-eagled and facing the sky. He lay there trying to lift himself before finally, unsteadily getting to his feet. He stood on shaky legs and called out to the hedgehog. "Now, find a place to hi—"

Ingot never finished the sentence.

The owl swept him up like a limp scrap of fur and began to carry him off to the clouds.

"Nooooooooo!" screamed Marcel, jumping up and chasing after Wickedwing's precious prey. Marcel felt himself reach for Scamp's old sling-shooter. Numbly, he looked around for a pebble, a scrap of brick, anything.

He grabbed a hunk of plaster but fumbled it. He tried a piece of splintered wood, put it in the pocket of the shooter, and hurled it toward the sky. It helicoptered down. Wickedwing climbed.

"This isn't how the movie ends!" he heard himself cry.

Marcel's eyes landed on the frozen pipe at the top of the rubble. A single icicle hung from the metal, glinting.

The Wizard of Oz. The Witch. Dorothy. The bucket of water.

It wasn't a bucket of water, but if water melted witches, maybe ice . . .

Marcel ran for the pipe, snapped off the icicle, placed it in the sling, and carefully took aim.

If he could wish on ruby slippers and fluorescent stars, if there was any magic to be called upon in this world, any prayer to be prayed, he did it now. He placed every hope he ever had in this one whisper: "Let me save him."

The sling drew back. The icicle gleamed with what he hoped was a deadly sheen. Marcel could still make out the limp brush of the squirrel's tail as he aimed. And fired.

The icicle shot through the air like a rocket set on course. Higher and higher it climbed until Marcel could no longer see the frozen arrow, so instead, he watched the owl.

The witch flew with determination, her powerful wings carrying Ingot to his grave. One beat of her wings. Two. And then—

Something rocked her to her side. Flapping frantically, she tried to steady herself and lost a few feet of sky. Ingot now dangled from one foot. Feathers flew. One fluttered down and settled just a few feet away. Marcel kept his eyes on the witch and wished and wished and wished.

Let me save him.

Let me save him.

Let me save him.

Wickedwing dropped a few feet, flapped. Dropped several feet more. Ingot swung dangerously from her sharp talons.

Not like this. Please, let me save him.

And all at once, the owl plummeted. End over end. Wings and claws and feathers.

Ingot, now free from her grasp, tumbled too.

With a great crash, Wickedwing fell into the ruins, still.

Ingot was falling, and Marcel ran to where he thought the squirrel might land. He wasn't sure he could catch him, but he had to try. If nothing else, he might break the squirrel's fall.

But Ingot landed before Marcel got there.

Into the folds of the great velvet curtain the squirrel went, snow exploding out as he hit. Marcel dashed up the mountain of wood and bricks and slid down the curtain to where Ingot lay. "Ingot! Ingot! Are you hurt? Please say you're okay!"

The squirrel's eyes were closed. His leg was bleeding heavily, and one shoulder looked a bit out of joint. Ingot gave a bubbly groan and answered with a growl. "I'm just peachy."

"Wickedwing—she's gone, Ingot. We don't have to worry! But we've got to get you help!"

Ingot let out a short, burbled laugh. "You've got good aim, kid. Real good. But don't hold your breath about me." His eyes remained shut. "I'm pretty broken up."

Marcel felt the tears well up. "Why did you do that? You're hurt! Why'd you try to rescue me?" he cried.

The squirrel's voice was low, the words slipping from his mouth, slow as the falling snow. "I rescued you, you rescued Toto, Tuffy rescued himself, and Scamp rescued everyone, Mousekinland, the whole entire world—a few times." Ingot snorted at his joke, and Marcel watched as all the squirrel's memories passed over his face.

The mouse's bluster and bravado.

Tuffy's innocent affection.

Marcel's friendship and how he, the hedgehog, had brought them all together on this, the most remarkable journey of the old squirrel's life.

A soft smile curled the corner of Ingot's mouth. "Lots of rescuing going on. But from the moment you barged into my tractor, you all rescued me."

Marcel shook his head angrily. "We should've let you be. We never should have asked you to help us! Look at you now!"

"I needed rescuing!" Ingot's voice was stern. "Angry and alone—what kind of life is that?" He closed his eyes. "I thought I had nothing left to live for after losing my family. I thought . . . I didn't realize—" His breath caught. "I was lost until you found me."

Marcel was crying angry tears. "But you'd be

okay! You wouldn't be hurt! What could you possibly have now that's worth this?"

Ingot was quiet. He opened a tired eye and looked at the hedgehog, his broken glasses, and the cocoon strapped tight to his chest. "My heart, Marcel. You found the little bit of heart I guess I had left in here." Ingot bumped a gentle fist on his chest. "You made it beat again." A smile crept to his lips. "What good is a heart if it doesn't beat for a thing?"

"I wished to save you," Marcel whispered. The snow swirled; the night deepened. "I only wanted to save you," he cried.

And Ingot, bruised and broken, looked at him then, with so much love. "Hedgehog, you did."

✦ ✦ ✦

Somewhere in the night, the old rusty heart of the squirrel beat its last.

He wasn't alone when it did.

CHAPTER 26

The Biggest, Most Beautiful Things

SNOWFLAKES KISSED INGOT'S FUR, AND A SMILE lay frozen on his lips as Marcel tucked the squirrel into the plush folds of the velvet curtain. Had he not known otherwise, Marcel would've guessed Ingot was only asleep and dreaming the most wonderful dream, the look of peace was so profound upon his face. And maybe he was.

Maybe some dreams—the best ones—don't end.

The night was somehow colder and so much darker now. Marcel couldn't bear the thought of staying there in the rubble of his old home—

now Ingot's final resting place. There seemed to be no choice.

And so he found himself back. Back on the streets.

Small and alone.

With a heart both more broken and more put together than it had been in a long time.

Loss always breaks you. But love—even love that spans miles and time—finds a way to mend the broken places. Scamp and Tuffy and poor Ingot—they would always be part of his heart.

But it was all that was still broken that stole most of Marcel's thoughts now. He missed Ingot. He missed the theater and the hens. He missed Scamp and Tuffy and . . .

Dorothy.

The streetlamps lit his way down the sidewalks, past darkened shops and restaurants, past a pet shop and a twenty-four-hour Laundromat, its machines humming away and a cloud of flowery perfume puffing into the air.

He didn't pay attention to where he was going. Tears blurred his eyes. Block after block slipped by, unnoticed. The snow came fast now, and the streets, every bench and fence post, every awning and car, wore a winter white.

The tinsel snowflakes hanging from the lampposts, the colored lights strung around bushes and doorways, the cheery pine trees in so many a window gave the streets a warm and stubborn glow, and Marcel despised it. He determined to stop in the darkest spot he could find.

Toto wriggled against his chest, and Marcel felt only a sliver of relief.

At least he wasn't *completely* alone.

"We'll stop soon, Toto," he said, tucking the leaf-sack around the cocoon to keep him warm.

It was a lie. They trudged through the snow for hours.

Ahead, the street came to a tee at a low brick wall. Beyond it, Marcel could make out the dark, shadowy silhouettes of trees.

A park, Marcel thought to himself, and as little light could be seen beyond its walls, it seemed the right—the only—place to stop.

Marcel had his pick of entrances, and he found the darkest, loneliest one he could find. A path wound through the trees, and he followed it. It ended in a lawn dotted with leafless bushes and bare oaks. The snow had stopped now, and the clouds rolled back. Without thinking much about it, Marcel continued on toward a large open space under the sky.

Toto was wriggling continuously now, and Marcel thought it strange. Maybe he'd been hurt after all. Marcel sat and unstrapped the cocoon and was shocked to find the cocoon peeling away from a small brown moth curled tightly inside.

"Toto!" shouted Marcel. "You're a moth! You're beautiful." He held the little moth carefully in his paws, making sure to give the creature space to shrug off its garments and shake out its wings.

For the next hour Marcel spoke softly to the moth as it rested and blood pumped into its wings. Marcel sheltered it from the cold as best he could, even blowing puffs of hot air over it so it wouldn't catch a sniffle. The moth stretched and fluttered, and Marcel felt himself a happier hedgehog, thankful again that he wasn't alone after all.

"I'll find you some flowers," Marcel told Toto. "Moths like flowers, don't they? Or is that butterflies? Scamp would know. But I'll help you find food—don't worry about that." Toto's wings opened and closed with ease, and he seemed to be listening, Marcel thought. How fortunate it was that he'd found the little cocoon a week ago!

Marcel supposed the moth must know of all he'd done to try to help him. And now Marcel felt Toto would surely offer him the same in return. Maybe not protection, but certainly companionship—the comfort of a friend. "We'll have so much fun come spring, I promise. It's not so cold then, and . . ."

Toto began to creep out from under the small shelter Marcel had made of his paws. "Wait. Don't do that, Toto," he chided. "It's cold and wet out there. You'll want to stay here, where it's warm and dry."

Toto appeared not to hear him and continued

to crawl farther, to the tips of Marcel's claws, fluttering his wings as he walked.

"It's terribly cold. Won't you come just a little closer out of the wind?" Marcel urged.

Toto fluttered his wings again and turned to fix his tiny black eyes on Marcel. The moth stood there a moment, and as the hedgehog watched through his cracked spectacles, Toto lifted his wings, turned, and slipped into the wind without a word.

"Totoooooooooo!" Marcel wailed, rushing after him. "Toto, come back! Don't leave me!"

But the small moth disappeared into the night in a blink.

It was all, finally, too much for Marcel. He dropped to his knees, sobbing.

He'd lost everything. Dorothy and the theater. The hen sisters—at least they had Gomer. And Ingot—he was somewhere over the rainbow now. Marcel sobbed as hard as he had that day in the park. The memories came back now to haunt him.

A summer day. A picnic blanket. A few grapes, some string cheese. A couple of warm bologna sandwiches with his Dorothy.

And then the arrival of a soccer ball and an invite from the blue-eyed boy to play.

Dorothy had nestled Marcel into her backpack and set him under a tree in the shade.

"You stay here," she'd said. "I won't be long. Stay here in the backpack and I'll come back in a little bit."

Marcel had listened. Begrudgingly.

For a little while anyway.

But dark thoughts began to creep in again.

Was Dorothy growing tired of him like the others had? Would it all end the same?

Was it just that every pet moved on eventually? Were fickle hearts just the way of the world? Was the best you could hope for a warm bed, a full bowl, and a theater seat in someone's heart . . . before the movie ended, the credits rolled, and the theater was swept clean to make ready for the next show?

Marcel had thought about the day so often since.

The boy, the bird, the bicycle basket, the basset hound.

After Dorothy had run off to join Ethan, the chirp of a bird drifted into Dorothy's backpack from somewhere close by, sounding exactly the way his heart felt: a bit broken.

Just a peek, he told himself. He'd poked his nose out of the backpack. *Just a quick peek.*

A small and fuzzy robin sat under a bush not ten feet away.

"Hello there," Marcel called out to her. "Are you all right?"

"Not really," she'd answered, hopping over to him and explaining the story of her absent parents, her empty nest, and those troublesome, terrible worms.

"That your nest there?" she'd asked, peering at the bicycle basket.

And that's when he'd seen it. The sign. The FOR SALE in bold lettering.

That's when the truth of the boy and the words

of the bird made their way to his heart. Dorothy had chosen Ethan over Marcel. It was just a matter of time before he was replaced completely in her heart. It hadn't taken long for Sweetie Jones. Would Marcel have a month? A week? A handful of days before he was pushed from the nest entirely?

"You can stick with me, if you want," said the bird. "We can look out for each other."

Now, to say that he'd been torn in that moment didn't quite do it justice. To say he was torn like a velvet curtain in the rubble of a destroyed theater would've been close.

He thought about Sweetie Jones, Ed, Darla Pickens, and Marty Henkle. He thought about the others and the Shirley River Animal Shelter.

I should go, said a voice inside him. *I should go before she does.*

And just like that, like the way a hard kernel instantly and irrevocably pops into a piece of popcorn, everything changed.

He'd crawled out of the backpack. He'd followed the bird across the field toward a large hedge of honeysuckle. He remembered looking back at Dorothy one last time. Seeing her braids fly behind her as she chased after the soccer ball. Seeing her give Ethan a playful nudge and dissolve into laughter.

She was so happy.

In the end, that's all he could've wanted for her.

And he disappeared into the bush.

He'd followed the bird through the honeysuckle. Past trees. Along a quiet path. At one point he thought he heard something. Far away. It almost sounded like . . .

Was that his name? Was Dorothy calling his name?

"Do you hear that?" he'd asked the bird. "I thought I heard Dorothy!" He felt dizzy. "I've made a mistake. I should go back!"

But the bird shook her head. "Oh no. You can't go back," she assured him. "Once you leave the nest, you can never go back. That's the rule."

Marcel hadn't had time to question it, for at

that very moment, a few kids on bicycles came whizzing down the path and nearly squashed him.

The bird fluttered under a park bench, and Marcel ran to hide himself in a rosebush. He was shaking. He crouched there hoping to blend into the thorns until he could make his way back to Dorothy's backpack. He'd made a mistake. He shouldn't have wandered.

But just then, a spaniel, sniffing around a tree not far away, hunting for whatever interesting smells he could find, caught a scent—a stick, a bug, a *hedgehog*. He began to bark, a shrill, excited bark that sounded exactly like a hungry one.

The dog tugged at his owner's leash and broke away.

And Marcel ran. He ran for what he thought was his life. Through bushes, around twisty paths, over rocks and boulders and leafy knolls. He ran until his legs buckled and his lungs gave out. He didn't know how long he'd run, how far he'd gone. He'd never even stopped to see if the spaniel had followed.

When he found himself in the middle of a thickly wooded part of the park, with no bird, no idea what direction he'd come from, and weak eyes that offered little help, Marcel tried to call for her.

"Dorothy! My Dorothy! Where are you?"

Somehow, she'll hear. Somehow, she'll find me, Marcel thought.

But she didn't hear. The old basset hound did.

"Don't worry. I won't eat you," the hound had said, when Marcel stumbled upon his hollow. And those few, kind words were all Marcel needed to spill everything that was in his heart. Everything from Sweetie Jones to shelters, to Dorothy and running away.

"I been there myself," the basset hound had said. "Fifteen different places and more stories than you can count. But it's better to forget all that. Put it all out of your mind. The past is the past. What's done is done. All there is, is now." He'd offered Marcel a place to stay for the night. "Been on my own a long time now, and you won't convince me there's anything better. But I don't mind a visitor now and then. Even strays get lonesome sometimes."

Marcel had thanked him for his hospitality but decided to go on. If Dorothy was out there, he'd do all he could to find her, and hope, *hope* there was still a way to get back.

It was just a little bit farther. A bit farther, a little longer. If he just kept going, he was sure to stumble upon their picnic blanket and the backpack.

But as the day wore on and dusk began to settle, as night crept in and the dew fell cold and cheerless upon his face, the dark trees, the screaming birds, and the wailing wind all seemed to say:

You are lost.

You're alone.

You'll never find your Dorothy again.

Never.

It was many days and countless city blocks before Marcel found the theater.

And it took time, but after a while, he felt himself fortunate. At least he had a couple of hens that loved him. And with *The Wizard of Oz* playing every Saturday matinee, there was hope, wasn't there? That maybe a freckled, auburn-haired girl with braces, braids, and high-tops would one day float down the aisles and sit in seat 24G or 15C, and he'd run to her, and life could be what it magically once was?

But Saturdays slip by.

Hope dies away.

The biggest, most beautiful things are always hardest to believe in.

He'd realized it that day on the roof.

When he saw her skateboard disappear around the corner, he *knew* he had a choice.

Would he follow? Even if it meant losing Dorothy all over again? What if he never found her?

Did he even *deserve* to?

It was easier to stay.

And soon *the boy, the bird, the bicycle basket, the basset hound* was the mantra he told himself. It was easier, too, to believe it was all true. That he'd been replaced by the boy; that the bird had been right and you can never go back; that a FOR SALE sign on a basket means a FOR SALE sign on a heart; that the basset hound was right—that what's done is done, the past is the past, and that all you have is now.

Marcel sat in the snow. Alone again. With no home. Nothing. Even Toto had left him.

He was back at the beginning.

"Moths can be fair-weather friends, you know," said a voice.

Marcel looked up and felt his heart leap.

It was Oona! Dear, good Oona.

"We can't seem to stop bumping into one another," she said. "Quite literally that first day when you knocked me out of the sky with your flying box. And since then, it seems all I need to do is find the loneliest place around and look for the glint of your glasses." The moth chuckled. "I'll admit, it's been hard to keep up. You do travel far."

Her wings, torn and a bit rumpled, were as

beautiful as ever as she fluttered to him. "Found yourself in a bit of a predicament again, have you?" she asked.

Marcel bit his quivering lip to keep from crying out and nodded.

"Oh, Marcel. You do have a way of getting into trouble."

The dam to Marcel's tears broke again, and he wailed. He told Oona of Scamp's goodbye and Tuffy's reunion. He told her about the theater and hens, about Wickedwing, Toto. About Ingot. Then he told her about Dorothy. His Dorothy.

His heart was like the million pieces of a broken-down theater when he said at last, "I'm lost, Oona. I'm so very lost."

Oona placed a comforting foot on his paw and looked at him fondly. "Marcel, don't you know?"

He shook his head. What else was there to know?

Oona gave him a small smile. "We're all a little lost before we're found."

Marcel stopped crying. He sniffled. "We are?" he asked shakily.

"Oh yes. I think so. But I'm sorry you're lost. I'll help if I can."

Marcel shook his head. "You can't. But thank you. Just being here is enough."

The moth's face changed then, and she looked at him intently. "Marcel, do you believe?"

"Believe what?" he asked.

"Marcel," she repeated. "Do you *believe*?"

Marcel knew what she was asking.

Did he believe he *could* be found.

Find me.

"You must believe it's possible," said Oona.

But Marcel *did* believe it was possible. That wasn't the problem.

Miracles happened all the time.

His Dorothy was a miracle.

And so was the theater, he supposed. He'd found it after gulping down that cup full of greenish soda, hadn't he? He may have gotten sick, but he'd have never found the theater otherwise. So, in a way, that cup full of soda was a miracle too.

The hen sisters arrived after he'd smashed that

green bottle and sent their poultry truck flying.

Scamp determining to help him once she'd seen the unnatural color of his lime Fruit Gems and heard his plight—that was a miracle too.

And they just happened upon Ingot in his hulk of a tractor. His silver and *green* hulk of a tractor.

Tuffy. That strange tree. Full of vines and moss and green as spring.

The *green t*owers of the popcorn factory.

The *green* balloon on the box truck.

Oona's green and glowing wings fluttering broken and beautiful before him now.

"Hope, Marcel. Not just belief. You have to hope."

Marcel's eyes brimmed with tears again as he looked down at his feet.

Hope. Such a tricky thing it was.

To put your hope in something so precious and risk being disappointed even one. More. Time. It felt like the hardest thing you could ever be asked to do.

"Do you know?" said Oona. "Moths like me have just one week—one week to be a moth! That's a lot of life to be lived in such a short time. And how impossible it is that just as you were starting your journey, I was starting mine!" Oona smiled. "I wanted a friend and there you were. You and your box." She chuckled. "I don't understand journeys. But I do know what keeps us taking the next step. Hope, Marcel. Come now. It only takes a little."

It only takes a little, he heard Dorothy say.

It only takes a little.

Oona's face brightened. "If you could wish for anything, if you could be anywhere at all right now, where would you be? Come on, Marcel! Where?"

Marcel straightened his shoulders as best he could. He made room in his chest. With everything he had, with what tiny faith he could sweep out of a dusty corner of his heart, he said those five hard but simple words, words he'd loved for a very long time now.

"There's no place like home."

Marcel looked at the sky full of stars. He looked at Oona.

She nodded encouragingly.

Pick a star. Make a wish. Say a prayer. Dare to hope.

He picked one. It wasn't the biggest. It wasn't the brightest. It was just one small star. And then he closed his eyes, fixed his mind on Dorothy—his Dorothy—and clicked his tiny heels one, two, three times.

(It couldn't hurt.)

"I want to go home. I want to go home. I want to go home," he whispered.

Marcel opened his eyes to Oona smiling at him. "There's no place like home," he said again.

"There certainly isn't."

Oona reached up and touched Marcel's broken glasses. Marcel took them off and set them down.

"Do things look a bit different?" Oona asked him.

They did. A little. His glasses were so scratched and broken they weren't much help anyway. But that's not what Oona meant.

She wanted to know: Did he *see* things differently?

He did.

Things felt different when you dared to hope the smallest hope.

"Now take a deep breath and look, Marcel," said Oona. "Look around you. What do you see? What's the next step?"

Marcel closed his eyes. He took a deep breath. He let it out and looked.

Things were fuzzy. They usually were.

He saw glowing snow. The moon. The outlines of trees. Across the open field he saw a wooded area, trees all mashed together, pitch black against the moonlight. Just a blob of darkness, really. Except for . . . *that.*

What it was he couldn't tell, but something with a strange greenish glow stuck out from the darkness. "What's that?" Marcel asked, taking a step toward it.

"Let's go see," Oona replied.

Marcel ran and Oona flew over the open field. The greenish thing took shape as they drew nearer. It was a sort of column, peculiar and glowing faintly—a tree trunk. Marcel slowed to a trot, then a walk. Five feet away, he halted.

There, in front of him, was a tree. A glowing tree.

A tree covered in glow-in-the-dark star stickers.

"Oona, it's . . ." Marcel crept up to it, reached out, and plucked a sticker from the tree. He held it in his paws. "It's *Dorothy*."

Beneath his feet, a star sticker shone. A few feet away another was gleaming through the snow. And then more. Running off into the distance.

A trail, Marcel thought. His heart skipped a beat.

"Go ahead," said Oona.

Marcel crept ahead to the next star, and the next.

It *was* a trail.

A trail back home.

"She never gave up," Marcel said, turning to look at Oona. His face beamed, and his voice was choked. "Thank you," he said. "For helping me. For being my friend. Oh, thank you."

"See? A friend is never far away." The moth's face was bright as she floated to him, the green of her wings lit with the first hint of dawn. "Go, Marcel, go! Go home!" she urged.

Oona left a tiny kiss on his cheek and fluttered into the coming light. She looked back at him one last time, smiled—and flew away.

Marcel watched her go.

And then he turned and looked at the way before him. He took a shaky step.

The stars stood out against the darkness. A path. A star-sticker trail.

And with that, he ran. Passing sticker after sticker, star after star. There was popcorn now too. Here and there a soggy piece. Stars and popcorn, popcorn and stars. Marcel's heart swelled as the trees flew past, and then lampposts, buildings, and streets. He felt as if everything, everything—every stick, every snowflake, every house and rock and tree, every single atom—urged him on.

Go, Marcel! Go home!

He didn't know how long he ran, how many stars he passed, but it felt like two hundred seconds and two hundred hours, a handful of stickers and a heap.

He was going to her. He was going home.

Then the streets became sort of familiar; the houses looked very much like ones he knew.

The stone birdbath in the garden.

The yellow brick town house, one window wild with five braying hounds.

The house with the rusty porch swing. The old man bundled and swinging with his morning cup of tea.

Then he saw it. The old maple with the tire swing.

Marcel slowed as he came near, a snowy hedge blocking his view.

He reached the last star before the hedge ended and the trail turned up a short walk. His heart beat fast. A lump caught in his throat. He rounded the corner.

In front of him, the last stars and popcorn kernels dotted a shoveled walk.

A walk to a clapboard house with a painted door.

An old soccer ball left in the lawn. And a skateboard.

A new red bike was propped against the bushes. A new bike with an old basket. A hedgehog-size basket right there on the handlebars.

Marcel walked the final few steps, legs shaky. His heart, weary and broken, was also mended and so full.

One star was all that remained.

Marcel stood on the step. He looked up with tears in his eyes to see the stars he loved so dearly, the stars he'd wished on so many a night, winking out from the ceiling behind a third-story window.

Pick a star, he heard his Dorothy say. *Pick a star.*

And oh, he did.

In the window, an overhead light clicked on, and the stars winked out. The sun was just coming up over the horizon and painting everything a peach light.

Marcel took a deep breath and lowered his bleary gaze to the waiting flap of the hedgehog door he'd passed through so many times and wiped his feet on the tired old mat. Its faded green letters read: WELCOME HOME.

"Welcome home," he whispered to himself.

A smile crept over his face.

And Marcel stepped inside at last.

Finale

OUTSIDE A PLAIN BUT CHEERFUL HOUSE, WITH windows that glint in the sun and glow after dark stands a tree. It's an old tree. Its branches spread wide. They're filled with tiny buds like little promises in spring; they clutch clouds of fire come fall. One holds up a tire swing. And there, in the tree's trunk, at just about the third-floor window, you'll find a generous hole.

Now, look closer.

Four pairs of masked eyes peer out of the hole. They're looking through an open window, straight into a star-filled room. It isn't the stars they're taken with. It's a small television, where a girl in sepia tones sings a song about a rainbow. Not one pair of masked eyes can look away, foremost, their father. He watches from behind them, his back pressed up against a bit of wallpaper: an old front page of the *Shirley River Herald*, two treasured handprints muddying up the edge.

Look closer still.

On the ledge of the window sits the newly elected mayor of Mousekinland. She's taken this trip a few times, hitching a ride on a popcorn delivery truck bound for the city. It isn't a safe trip, but a foolhardy journey never bothered her much anyway. This time she's brought six mouselings, each one carrying a sling-shooter, each one quivering with barely controlled electricity. At this very moment, these normally wild and tiny mice can't seem to take their eyes away from the television either.

(It's probably safer that way.)

Now look.

Inside the starry room, on a bed with fourteen pillows, a few books, and a laptop sits a girl. She's a little older now. She still wears red high-tops, though, and a smile—a straight one, the braces long gone.

The girl sings her heart out for probably the millionth time as she watches her favorite movie on the television. Something about bluebirds and lemon drops and wishing upon stars and finding a land where dreams come true.

Next to her rests a giant bowl.

Of popcorn.

On the other side of the bowl sits a hedgehog, wearing a brand-new pair of spectacles and the heartiest of smiles.

And as he looks upon his Dorothy, I think you'll find—

He's singing his heart out too.

Acknowledgments

FIRST, I'D LIKE TO THANK THE ACADEMY . . .

Wait. Wrong speech.

To the team at Aladdin: I couldn't be more grateful. To Kristin Gilson, my editor, thanks for picking up a hitchhiker and guiding Marcel's story on its journey to publication. Jennifer Bricking, who once again did the most breathtaking cover, thank you! To everyone who's been working in the wings: Mara Anastas, Sara Berko, Valerie Garfield, Tiara Iandiorio, Michelle Leo, Jenny Lu, Brian Luster, Elizabeth Mims, Karin Paprocki, and Caitlin Sweeny. We share this stage, so come take a bow. It's greatly deserved. *Bravo!*

And a special thanks to the ever-effervescent Tricia Lin. My books were lucky to be in your hands. Thank you for rolling out the red carpet. I miss our smoked salmon breakfasts already.

Rena Rossner, my blockbuster agent. Remember how I always tell you what I'm working on and then send you something different? Thanks for not firing me. (I'll probably do it again.)

Cindy Baldwin, Jessica Vitalis, and Brian Montanaro, thank you for making Marcel's a better story with your keen eyes and expert critiques. If I had one, I'd share my Oscar with you.

My five-star writing community: #TeamMascaraTracks, Central/Western NY SCBWI, Pitch Wars pals, my 2019 debut partners, and Hope*writers—the friendship, support, and wealth of knowledge you bring to my table can't be put into words. And to the stars of JPST: Chris Baron, J. Kasper Kramer, Rajani LaRocca, Josh Levy, Gillian McDunn, Naomi Milliner, and Nicole Panteleakos, you are a daily joy. Workshopping under-the-sea mysteries and Three Bears retellings with you is an honor (and a hoot); celebrating every victory and commiserating the hard times together is a gift. You're my favorite kind of people.

To my beloved friends and family who keep me sane and laughing, I love you forever. And ever and ever and ever. You know who you are.

To all the artists who do the good work of putting hope and truth, beauty, and just. great. art. out there before and beside me, thank you. This book would never have been brought into existence without books and movies like *The Wizard of Oz* or *Leap* (whose character Mathurin inspired Marcel), or songs like "Over the Rainbow," and strangely enough, Ed Sheeran's energizing "Castle on the Hill" which I played on repeat during the 8,672 *Annie Jr.* musical rehearsals I wrote through in an elementary school cafeteria filled with budding thespians and one earnest director. And if you want the soundtrack to this book? Listen to Lauren Daigle's "Rescue," followed closely by "Love Like This." In fact, you can probably skip the book and just listen to those two songs. They say everything

I wanted and tried to. I found them at a crucial moment in the writing of Marcel's story. Moments like that keep you writing when everything in the world tells you to quit. I didn't quit. And those songs will forever stay the anthem of my heart.

Lastly, to every reader out there still finding their way home, keep going.

It's out there. Whether you find it, or it finds you, your WELCOME HOME is coming.

I'll tell 'em to brush off the mat.

About the Author

CORY LEONARDO IS AN INTERNATIONALLY PUBLISHED author of children's books (the very best kind). She loves movies and snooping around magical old theaters, but most days you'll find her reading and writing at a coffee-stained kitchen table, sweeping cookie crumbs from her keyboard. She lives in Baldwinsville, New York, with her husband, her three children, and a naughty, bow-tie-wearing bulldog named Truman.